Frederick William Robinson

Coward conscience

Vol. II.

Frederick William Robinson

Coward conscience
Vol. II.

ISBN/EAN: 9783337014100

Printed in Europe, USA, Canada, Australia, Japan

Cover: Foto ©Andreas Hilbeck / pixelio.de

More available books at **www.hansebooks.com**

COWARD CONSCIENCE.

BY

F. W. ROBINSON,

AUTHOR OF

"GRANDMOTHER'S MONEY," "LITTLE KATE KIRBY,"
&c., &c.

"O coward conscience, how dost thou afflict me!"
SHAKSPEARE.

IN THREE VOLUMES.

VOL. II.

LONDON:
HURST AND BLACKETT, PUBLISHERS,
13, GREAT MARLBOROUGH STREET.
1879.

LONDON ·
PRINTED BY DUNCAN MACDONALD,
BLENHEIM HOUSE.

CONTENTS

OF

THE SECOND VOLUME.

———

BOOK II.—LIKE FATE!

(CONTINUED.)

CONTENTS.

BOOK III.—MISERERE.

BOOK II.

LIKE FATE!

VOL. II.

COWARD CONSCIENCE.

CHAPTER X.

VIOLET HILDERBRANDT.

MISS HILDERBRANDT rose as Tom Dagnell approached her, and then, as if weak and ill, sank back into her seat. It was a beautiful face into which he gazed, but the brightness of it was not that of the early morning when they had crossed together from Honfleur to Littlehampton. There was hope upon it then, despite the uncertainty of the future; now, one might have thought that the expression, however *spirituelle*, was of utter despair.

Tom held his hand towards her, and she put hers within it readily. It was a greeting as of old friends; observers—had there been any—might have thought so to have seen this meeting. He was glad to discover her, and she rejoiced in her heart that he had come so far to be of service.

He sat down by her side, and said—

"At last we meet."

"Yes, at last," she murmured.

"You were in danger, and you came here after receiving my message?" he inquired.

"Yes. A lady to whom I have given a few music lessons was invited to this party to-night. I asked her to allow me to accompany her. I had a hope," she added, "you would call here in the first instance, to receive my thanks for all your kindness—all your interest in me. You, a stranger, too!"

"Don't say a stranger, please," said Tom, quickly, "I cannot regard *you* as a stranger. I am interested in your life, and in the danger by which you are threatened."

"Ah! yes," she said, with a little shudder. "I was in sore need of a friend, Heaven knows, and I could only think of you."

"What has been your trouble?" said Tom. "Tell me in what way I can be of service."

"Yes,—one moment."

She stopped to consider, or to frame into words some explanation of which she was afraid. The white gloved hands clasped themselves together, and the head drooped strangely —it was a fair picture in that cool retreat from the heat and bustle of the ball-room, and the subdued light from the Chinese lanterns above them seemed to be in harmony with the scene, and with the nature of their thoughts. She did not speak for several moments, and Tom Dagnell was content to wait. He was no longer impatient; she was discovered; the secret was at an end; the knight-errant had arrived to the rescue of the fair afflicted, and all was well now. It was pleasant to sit and watch the varying play of emotion on her features—it was the old times again, he thought. The old times! Only a few weeks had inter-

vened since their last, their first meeting—and
yet they were like old times, to look back at
the voyage by the Honfleur steamer, and to
remember what thoughts were in the minds of
each of them then. He had lived an age since;
he had made peace with his father, stepped from
poverty to wealth, been welcomed home, found
a mother and brother ready to receive him, and
Cousin Ursula prepared to take him for her husband. And Violet Hilderbrandt, what had been
her history? he wondered.

She spoke at last, and in answer to his
question.

"You ask me in what way you can be of
service to me, Mr. Dagnell," she said. "I will
tell you frankly, if you will not press me too
much with questions in return."

Tom inclined his head as if in half assent.
Here were the "unknown" and the "mysterious" rising up again—was he never to be free
from them?

She took a long deep breath, and then said in
a low tone—"I am being pursued, and I must
keep in hiding!"

" This is free England, Miss Hilderbrandt," Tom replied, " and there is no power in anyone to put a restraint upon your action."

" Ah! pardon me," she said, with a sigh, " but there is. That is the one awful thought by which I am haunted—from which I cannot escape."

" Then——"

" I can hardly be explicit now. I may never have the courage to tell you all," said Miss Hilderbrandt, more hurriedly and with more excitement, " but you may guess how hard I was beset, to think of you."

It was scarcely complimentary, but her listener said, and with a half-bow again,

" Yes, I can guess that. For you told me you would not write under any circumstances."

" I could not foresee these," she answered, sadly and apologetically. " I was being hemmed in—this place was new and foreign to me—and I felt that a strong brave hand, a shrewd clear head, could only help me at such a pass as mine. Ah! sir—all very selfish of me, and inconsiderate for you, but I knew not what to do."

"I am only too glad to be here," said Tom, "tell me in what way—or in any way—I can be of assistance."

"I have suffered much in sending for you. I feel a strange hypocrite of a woman sitting in your friend's house, and affecting to be calm and at my ease when I am half mad with suspense and horror. At any moment," she continued, her hand trembling as for an instant it was laid nervously upon his arm, "they may come in there—through that door and take me away!"

She shivered, and the fair young face seemed cut in marble for a while.

"Courage, Miss Hilderbrandt—you alarm yourself unnecessarily, I am sure," said Tom.

He was perplexed; the warning of the man whom he had met upon the sands at Littlehampton, who had tracked them to Birmingham, vibrated in his ears again. "*She is mad! She is in no way accountable for her actions—she is the victim of illusions which are gaining strength with every day !*" Was this—could this be the possible solution to it all? He did not think so for more than an instant—looking into her thoughtful face was looking into a fair page of woman's history.

" When I parted with you at Littlehampton," she continued, in the same low voice, "I did not have these fears. I had left home because——" she paused, and then went on again—" because home was unhappy, and I was best away from it. 'Here is the end of it,' I thought, 'I will begin my life afresh in England, and forget all but the mother.' My fears were only of the world before me,—this world—and I thought they would not be sorry I had gone away, after they had had time to think of it. I believed," she added, very thoughtfully, " that they would have left me to myself from that day—caring but little for me."

" And who are ' they '?" asked the listener.

" My father and his friends, or the people whom he calls his friends," she replied.

Tom did not tell her at once that he had met her father; he preferred to listen quietly, and to follow, if possible, the clue to her young life.

"They can do you no harm," Tom repeated. "You are your own mistress in England. It would require a strong motive for any interference with you?"

"It is a strong motive," she answered.

"You will not trust me with your story," said Tom, regretfully, "you will not tell me what this motive is?"

"No, impossible!" she cried.

"Not even that portion of it which bears upon the reason for your message to me?" he answered, paying no heed to her excitement. "I am to fight for you in the dark?"

"Yes, yes," she answered, "though you might be a better friend and of more help to me, if I could trust you."

Tom's face darkened quickly, and her keen womanly instinct saw that she had pained him.

"You forget there is no reason why I should wholly trust you, Mr. Dagnell," she said, gently. "I have seen you but once in my life. On that occasion you were interested in me, and proffered me your help. Well, sir, if you will help me now to get from Birmingham—get away anywhere—so that I may not be traced again. I will thank you very much. I will be grateful for your kindness, I will remember you for ever as the one true friend I have had. But don't ask me for my history. It will only pain and shock you."

"No."

"It will set you against me."

"On my honour—no!"

"I could not explain everything. I should not expect you to put faith in me," she continued. "It is not the same story even which I could have related to you last March. It has become lurid and threatening. I feared danger then so slightly that I never thought to change my name in coming here, or that there was need for a disguise in leaving them for good. But I was mistaken, God knows! I was very much mistaken."

"Well, well, I will not implore you for your confidence, Miss Hilderbrandt," said Tom, "and I will wait patiently for your confidence. I *am* only a stranger at present, and you are right to be on guard against me. But at least," he added, "I will trust *you*—with all my heart."

"Thank you," she murmured, with tears suddenly swimming in her dark eyes, "I will not be ungrateful. And," she added, after another minute's reflection, " there will be less mystery between us soon."

" I am glad of that. For you may remember that I hate mystery," Tom confessed. " I have been fighting against it for the last five weeks."

" With every day I shall be gathering strength to tell you something of my life, and you will be learning to know me as I am, and not with this poor glamour round about me."

With every day! She spoke as if she were to be the companion of him for all time now, as if from that hour dated a new and closer intimacy between them. What could he think of that? and what would Ursula Dagnell think of it presently?

CHAPTER XI.

THE END OF THE SOIRÉE.

MANY men as unsuspicious as Tom Dagnell, as ready as he to take upon trust the first confession of a pretty woman, would have hesitated as to the expediency of the next step, and resented, if not by speech, at least by action, the want of confidence which had been displayed on her side. But our hero was a man who trusted with his whole heart; he had told her that he would do so only a few minutes since, and it was not in his nature—he thought, scarcely in human nature—to doubt the earnestness of this fair girl's intentions.

She was in trouble—in danger, but she

shrank from stating at present what the danger was. He could save her from it without humiliating her by a revelation; she had wished for his consideration, his mercy in this matter, and he had agreed to it. The compact was signed and sealed between them. It was necessary now to act, and that speedily.

The morning on the Littlehampton sands recurred to him, and the time seemed to have come with it, now that she was more composed, to relate his own story.

"I saw your father this morning," he remarked.

The colour left her face again, and she turned with a new eagerness to listen.

"My father; did he say he was my father?" she inquired.

"Yes."

"It would not follow that that should be the truth," she said, very thoughtfully. "Will you describe him, please?"

Tom did so, to the best of his ability.

"Yes, it is he," she answered; "he is in England, then, with the rest?"

“ Pardon me—with——”

She hastened to interrupt him.

“ Now tell me what he said to you. All that he said to you. Remember, you must have no secrets from me !”

“ That is hardly fair,” said Tom, half reproachfully, “ but here are the facts of the case. They will show you what is going on—they will put you on your guard.”

“ Yes, I hope so,” she replied.

Tom Dagnell quickly detailed the adventures of the day, commencing from the advent upon the scene of Mr. Hilderbrandt, and concluding with his own journey to Birmingham, and the difficulties he had had to elude the vigilance of those by whom he was watched. Violet Hilderbrandt listened attentively. When he had finished, she said,

“ You did not wait for my telegram before beginning to act in my cause. You thought there was danger when you telegraphed to your brother ?”

“ Yes.”

“ It was kind to think of me,” she murmured; "I am grateful to you, Mr. Dagnell."

"Don't say a word more," entreated Tom. "I was anxious to act in your defence in some way."

"Thank you. And now,"—she paused again, and looked steadily at him—"did you believe I was mad, the victim of a delusion, in going away from home?"

"I did not believe a word your father said," answered Tom, very frankly; "it struck me at once that he was an awful liar, and—never mind —forgive me, please, he *is* your father, after all."

"Yes," she replied, sorrowfully, "he is! Strange that we both have had to look for troubles from our fathers. When I can think less selfishly, breathe more freely, you must tell me something of your present life."

"It is common-place enough," was Tom's reply. "The prodigal has returned; the fatted calf has been killed—and there is peace at Broadlands."

"And happiness?" she asked, as if led ·on to consider his affairs, despite herself.

" Yes—just as you prophesied there would be."

She shrugged her shoulders in the foreign fashion which he had noticed once before in her, and said,

" I am the worst of prophets—but I am glad that I was right for once. And now—" darting at a tangent from the topic to which she had been led—" how can I get away from here? —in what way can I elude the spies who are coming thick and fast upon me?"

" You must not return to Bath-row."

" It will not be safe," she answered. " My mother urged me to get away at once."

" You are in communication with your mother?"

" Yes, when it is possible."

" Is she aware your father is spreading abroad a report of your insanity?" asked Tom.

" He is not doing so," answered Violet Hilderbrandt. " No one has ever said or thought of that. It was the impulse of the moment on his part to deceive you—to interest you in the ' father,' and throw you off your guard."

"Mr Hilderbrandt is a tolerably artful customer," said Tom, reflectively.

"He is an actor—a few years ago he might have been a great actor."

"Has he been a clerk in a London firm?"

"I do not know. It is likely. He has been everything," she replied.

"Has he——"

"You must not cross-question me," she said, with a faint smile, "remember you must wait my time to tell you all. Here is Miss Oliver."

The lady in the pink silk and white lace was before them, and Marcus Dagnell was seen also approaching leisurely from the ball-room.

"My dear Miss Hilderbrandt, I have been looking for you everywhere," the lady said, and Tom thought this was scarcely a correct statement, "and you will forgive my intrusion on your *tête-à-tête*; but, if you will kindly play once more, only once more before we separate, we should be so very much obliged! Papa and mamma beg that you will favour us—pray do!"

"The hour is very late,—Miss Hilderbrandt

is fatigued," said Tom, answering for her.

"I know it is very selfish of us," said Miss Oliver, still urgently. "That it is not in rule, at a dance,—that we are all very rude and encroaching with our provincial manners; but then Miss Hilderbrandt is a genius whom we are not fortunate enough to secure every day. You will favour us—I know you will," she exclaimed, clapping her gloved hands together.

"Yes, I will play if you wish," said Miss Hilderbrandt, rising.

"Oh! how kind of you," cried Fanny Oliver, wreathing one arm round the waist of Miss Hilderbrandt. "How good of you, to be sure! Mr. Dagnell," shaking her head archly at our hero, "you will never forgive my intrusion, but they were all dying to hear Miss Hilderbrandt again."

"I would sooner they had died than worried her like this, Marcus," said Tom roughly, as the ladies passed from the conservatory. "Cannot Miss Oliver, cannot any of you, see that Miss Hilderbrandt is unwell? Why should she play to amuse these people?"

"She is really a great pianiste, Tom," said Marcus. "Slitherwick tells me that he has heard her abroad, dozens of times, I think he said; but I wasn't listening attentively. I can't listen to Slitherwick very attentively, somehow. He is an awful bore."

"Yes, he looks like it," answered Tom, absently.

Meanwhile Miss Hilderbrandt had been led to the grand piano, and the guests, still disinclined to go home, thronged round her immediately.

"It's so very kind of you," said Fanny Oliver. "I don't know how we shall ever thank you enough—I don't, indeed! And perhaps you hate me already?"

All this in an undertone whilst searching for some music in a portfolio. Miss Hilderbrandt glanced at Miss Oliver, inquiringly.

"Hate you!—why?" she asked.

"I took you from *him*, you know—and he will never forgive me. I saw revenge on his countenance," said Fanny. "Oh! he has been so dreadfully cross."

Miss Hilderbrandt looked at the music which had been tendered her, and did not answer. There was no response needed, and it was not in her power to give one, had it been requisite.

It was strange, she thought, that Thomas Dagnell should be set down so quickly as her lover—she who had had no time for love in all her busy life—she who had only guessed at what love might be! She was vexed to think this light, chattering young lady at her side should have quickly taken for a fact that which had no existence save in her own frivolous brain; but there was no time to deny, or assert, or defend herself. In the house of the dish-cover merchant there was a part to assume, and she must go on with it at any cost to her feelings.

She touched lightly the keys of the piano, and drifted into melody—strange and complicated and full of wild sweet sounds which held one spell-bound at the witchery of the music, and the consummate skill of the player.

Yes, this was no amateur, thought Tom, rather a genius, leagues away from the honourable body of respectable incapacity. Here was one who loved music, and made it part, and the greater part, of her existence; who lived for it, and by it, and had already become celebrated by its practice. Tom possessed but little musical knowledge, but he was spell-bound with the rest of the guests. He could see the members of the little orchestra whom Mr. Oliver had engaged for his ball poised on tiptoe, and craning their necks to catch a glimpse of the fingering; the guests stood in one silent compact crowd of listeners—there was more than one visitor transfixed and open-mouthed; it reminded Tom of the old legends of the power of sound, from which story-books and operas have had more than one theme. At the conclusion, there was a rapturous burst of applause, as though a theatre or opera-house had been the scene of Miss Hilderbrandt's performance; but it was a genuine and unaffected compliment to the player, if hardly in the best taste. The pianiste was, however, insensible to her success, the trial had been too great, the day's excitement and suspense too acute; and she had hardly risen, pale and trembling, from the instrument, when she closed her eyes and fell back into the arms of Miss Oliver.

There was confusion in the ball-room, and Miss Oliver, always at high pressure, began to scream.

"She's dead, I'm sure she's dead. Oh! Mr. Slitherwick, pray assist me!"

Mr. Slitherwick rushed forward to take Miss Hilderbrandt from Miss Oliver's embrace, when he was unceremoniously thrust aside by Tom Dagnell, a gentleman also on the *qui vive*, and generally a trifle impulsive.

"Stand back, please, don't press round her!" he demanded, sternly; "you should have had more consideration for this lady, all of you, than to have asked her to play. You could see how ill she was—open the windows, Marcus, or smash them open, will you?"

"No, no, don't smash anything," shouted Mr. Oliver, in alarm. "God bless my soul, what an extraordinary young man! The conservatory is the nearest, and all the sashes slide, Mr. Dagnell, on the newest principle. You can get as much air as you like there."

Tom lifted his fair burden and carried her off to the conservatory, followed by many sympathising ladies and gentlemen. In the cooler retreat, with windows open and the morning air blowing in upon her, Miss Hilderbrandt came quickly to herself.

"Did I faint away?" she asked, looking hard at Tom. "Have I really been insensible?"

Tom answered in the affirmative.

"How I detest a scene," she said; "they must have thought I did it on purpose. For theatrical effect, probably," she added, a little scornfully.

"Nonsense! They are not uncharitable people here. In fact, they have nearly smothered you with their sympathy. Besides," said Tom, "you looked like death itself."

"Like death itself!" she repeated, slowly. "Ah, if it had been!"

"You must not leave us to-night, Miss Hilderbrandt," cried Fanny Oliver, foremost on the scene again. "You must not fatigue yourself any more. I insist upon it; papa and mamma insist upon it, and Mrs. Damper, I am sure, will excuse your returning with her. Will you not, Mrs. Damper?"

Tom answered at once, both for Mrs. Damper and Miss Hilderbrandt. He seized the advantage which Violet Hilderbrandt's sudden indisposition had offered.

"It will be the better plan," he said. "Thank you, Miss Oliver, it is very kind and considerate of you. She will stay, I am sure she will."

"If I should not be troubling you too much," said Violet Hilderbrandt, "I—I should be glad to remain to-night."

"Troubling us! Why, we've as many spare rooms as a hospital!" cried Mr. Oliver from the rear, "and we are only too proud of so distinguished a guest, ma'am, I assure you."

Violet murmured her thanks, and then sat back in her chair with half-closed eyes.

"You would like to get away from this?" said Tom, in a whisper, "you are tired and weak?"

"Yes. I should be glad to rest," she murmured.

Fanny Oliver was quick to respond, and a

few minutes afterwards Violet Hilderbrandt was moving from the ball-room with her.

"Good night," Violet said to Tom Dagnell, extending her hand to him, "and thank you very much."

She left him to guess at that which she was thanking him for; it was for all interest and fore-thought in her service, he knew, and Tom bowed low over the cold, little hand which had been left in his for a moment, like a gentleman of the old school.

"I shall see you to-morrow," he said.

"Yes," was her answer, "early to-morrow I shall be stirring, I hope, or rather," she corrected, "early to-day."

"I had forgotten the day was upon us," answered Tom.

"Yes, another day!" she said.

Violet Hilderbrandt and Fanny Oliver departed, and it was the signal for a rapid dispersion of the guests. They were busy with the carriages in the front of Hagley-road; there was a great deal of calling and shouting without, which woke up Cabbage, who began barking vigorously for the next quarter . of an hour; there were farewells between guests and host, and between the guests themselves even a few fond, foolish promises, born of ball-room programmes; the musicians packed up their instruments and took their fees and parting glasses, and the daylight was very bright and strong now, and could not be hidden away. The market carts were coming in from the country, and a milkman, a policeman, and one or two stragglers stood on the other side of the road, interested in the visitors as they were whirled homewards in their various equipages.

Tom remained in the hall watching the guests depart, or anxious for the fresh morning air that came in through the open doorway, where one or two of the servants were posted also, looking sharply out for shillings.

"Safe for this time, at least, and time to think of the next step," Tom muttered, in a half soliloquy.

"I beg pardon, what did you say?" inquired Marcus, who was at his elbow.

"Nothing particular; I was musing *a la* Hamlet," replied his brother.

"*A la* Bravo of Venice it sounded to me—something about being safe for the time, wasn't it?"

"It was," Tom confessed, "but you shouldn't listen, Marcus,—it's a bad habit."

"I never listen to anything, 'pon my honour, Tom," said Marcus, slowly. "I was coming to ask you if you would oblige us all by slipping into Cabbage with a stick for half a minute; he's kicking up a most confounded row."

"Let him be."

"He'll wake the whole house up next," said Marcus, "there's Miss Hilderbrandt and Fan——"

"Oh, by Jove! yes, we must stop his noise—a word will do it," and Tom went round with alacrity to the stables. The great side gates were wide open to the street—people who had come long journeys had availed themselves of Mr. Oliver's range of stabling and put up their horses and carriages for a while, and taken them away again, leaving the gates open.

After a word of remonstrance with Cabbage, Tom glanced out at the open street. The carriages were thinning fast, the loiterers had gone, only the policeman and the milkman were still curious. The birds were singing in the big trees in front of the house, the sun was shining, the sky was blue and faintly flecked with soft white clouds. Tom looked up at the sky, as if interested in the weather for the day, glanced across the road, and then turned away.

" They've had a swell kick up there," said the milkman to the policeman, " I wish I had a quarter of the money they've chucked away to-night."

" Ah !" replied the policeman, with a grin, " it would have done us a sight more good."

"Right you are, guv'nor, in that," said the milkman, poising his pails and preparing to depart on his rounds. " That's Mr. Owen's crib, isn't it ?"

" I don't know any Owens in Hagley Road."

" Whose place is it, then ?"

"Mr. Oliver's, to be sure."

"Ah! I don't have his custom—I wish I did."

"You're a new hand altogether about here," said the officer. "How long have you had this walk?"

"I've just been taken on by Simpson," was the reply.

The milkman went away after this response. He did not care to be questioned himself—it depressed him seriously, coming as it did from an official quarter. He inclined his head thoughtfully from that moment, and directed two small black eyes towards the ground.

"Oliver's—Elmslie House," he muttered twice to himself, as he proceeded on his way. "I think we've run the fox to earth at last."

CHAPTER XII.

COMING EVENTS.

VIOLET HILDERBRANDT had resolved upon rising early the day after the party —had indeed given instructions to be called early, as though some project for a speedy departure from Elmslie House were already on her mind, but in her plans she had miscalculated her own strength. It was close upon eleven in the morning when she awoke for the first time; all the better and stronger for the complete rest that she had had. Life was hardly steeped in the same dull grey tints this bright May morning; she was with friends; she was not entirely alone, there was one to trust in her implicitly. Tom Dagnell had said so only a few hours ago, and it was pleasant to be trusted at last, and

by a man who had wandered about the world
and run away from home after her own fashion
—but yet with what an awful difference !

As she opened her eyes, a neatly-clad young
woman rose from a chair before the fire, which
was burning in the grate.

"If you please, ma'am, I am Miss Oliver's
maid. Miss Oliver said 1 was to wait here till
you awoke, and assist you to anything you
might require," said the attendant.

"Miss Oliver is very kind," replied Violet,
"but 1 am not accustomed to assistance, and
will excuse you, with my thanks."

"Very well, madam," was the answer. "Miss
Oliver told me to light the fire, as you might
find the room chilly this morning, she thought
—and if you please, Miss Oliver's compliments,
and begs that you will make use of this costume for the present," holding up an elaborate
morning robe.

"I shall not require it," said Violet. "My
compliments to your mistress, and I would
prefer the dress I wore last night."

"Very well, ma'am."

It was a rich black silk—"high-bodied," we believe is the term—which Miss Hilderbrandt had worn at the ball, but it was simple enough for morning costume, being destitute of trimming, and even severely classic in its utter absence of ornamental detail. She was dressed when Miss Oliver came into the room, all puffs and flounces.

"You have slept well, my dear Miss Hilderbrandt; you are quite sure you have slept well?" Fanny Oliver inquired, after kissing Violet affectionately. "I gave the strictest instructions for the servants to be very quiet in the passages, and I have been watching like a lynx to make sure that my commands were scrupulously obeyed."

"I have slept very well, thank you," replied Miss Hilderbrandt.

"I am so glad! You are looking better, too—you are quite yourself again. *He* has been asking after you," said Fanny, meaningly.

"He?" repeated Violet Hilderbrandt.

"Mr. Tom Dagnell, to be sure," said Fanny.

"He was very cross last night, and said it was

all our fault that you fainted; but he has forgiven me, as I hope you have, dear."

"I have nothing to forgive. - I am subject to
these fainting fits, at times. It would have happened at home, if not here," said Violet.

"Ah! he did not tell us that," said Fanny.
"He said it was all our barbarity, in forcing you
to play when you were weak and ill. He said
all kinds of things; he pushed Mr. Slitherwick
over a foot-stool, because he was going to support you, and he asked Marcus to smash all the
windows for air. In fact, Miss Hilderbrandt, he
lost his reason when his lady-love swooned, as
he was in duty bound to do."

Fanny Oliver was very arch that morning—
extremely arch,—but her listener did not recip-
rocate her tone. The face into which Fanny
had looked laughingly, had become almost as
grave as last night's.

"I cannot account for Mr. Dagnell's excitement," Violet said, calmly.

"I like him very much—I do indeed," said
Fanny, misunderstanding her, "though I had
not seen him since I left boarding-school, until

last night. You have known him a very long while. I suppose you met abroad?—Tell me all about it, pray·do!"

" About what? I do not understand, I am afraid."

" Oh! but you do," said Fanny, with a peal of laughter far from unmusical, " and I, of course, am deeply interested. Why, we may be sisters soon, think of that! For Marcus and Tom are brothers, you know, and I am engaged to Marcus; why, it's a complete little family circle."

. Miss Hilderbrandt regarded her companion with amazement. Fanny's rapid utterance, the quickness with which she dashed to a conclusion, framed her own version of the story, and commented upon it as a fact that was real and indisputable, was subject matter for no little wonderment and fear. She hastened to set Fanny right.

" You are in error, Miss Oliver," she said. " Pray consider you are very much in error, and may cause me serious embarrassment. Mr.

Dagnell I saw last night for the second time in my life."

"Indeed. Oh! how strange—how romantic —how you *have* got on!" cried Fanny, "I am more curious than ever, now."

"Mr. Dagnell is nothing to me—can be nothing at any time," said Violet, still hurriedly, and even nervously. "We are chance acquaintances, whom a chance accident of life has brought together strangely. That is all."

"I don't believe in chance," said Fanny Oliver, with wonderful impressiveness. "I believe in Fate. Don't you?"

"I try not," answered Violet, "for I have been fighting against Fate all my life."

"I like Fate so much better myself. It saves a deal of trouble. But don't they want you to marry him, or do they want him to marry some one else?" she asked, eagerly.

Violet Hilderbrandt wished that she had not spoken of Fate, the instant after the word had escaped her; this demonstrative, good-tempered, inconsiderate, and thoughtless girl clung so persistently to her first wild theory.

"I was not thinking of Fate in connection with Mr. Dagnell," said Violet.

"Ah! but there is something very strange going on at Broadlands," said Fanny, "and Marcus thinks he is keeping it cleverly from me, but oh! no, he isn't. He tells me he promised not to say anything about his brother Tom to me, or anyone, before he left Sussex. What was that for?"

"I cannot explain," said Violet.

"I asked who made him promise, and what was the reason for it; but, oh! dear, he's so stupid. I couldn't get any sense out of him. Still, this is my impression, that——"

"Stay, stay," said Violet, interrupting her, "do not tell me anything about your friends, Miss Oliver, please. I am a stranger to them, remember. They will not like your canvassing their merits and demerits to me. I am quite sure they will not."

Miss Oliver stopped at last, after this urgent protest.

"Well, not to-day, then," she said, "although it cannot matter between you and me, that I

can see. Only I am keeping you from your breakfast, which I have had laid in my own boudoir,
so that I shall have you all to myself, just for a
little while longer. Am I not a designing
young person, to have planned all this whilst
you were sleeping ?"

"You are very kind to think of me," said
Violet.

She would have preferred that Miss Oliver
had thought a little less of her; for these at-
tentions, kind. and well-meant as they were,
rendered her nervous and confused. The Birmingham heiress might become a woman to
love in time, and with time to study her; but
her chirruping garrulity, even her anxiety to
please and to become her friend, almost at first
sight, served to deter Violet Hilderbrandt
rather than draw her towards her. Violet was
in a new, strange world, and was only there on
sufferance; she could not look lightly upon it
through the mists by which she was surrounded. She was a woman in danger, as Tom
Dagnell had already asserted, and, moreover,
she was a woman on guard.

The manufacturer's daughter led the way to her boudoir; bright and radiant with all the gilding and colour which money could supply, and where a sumptuous breakfast awaited them. Here Violet Hilderbrandt was set more at ease by Miss Oliver's ordinary subjects of discussion, and had she been open to flattery, or not too well accustomed to it, it was possible that the rapt admiration of her companion might have turned her head a little.

"If you would only give a *matinée* in Birmingham, I should die happy," ran on this exuberant young lady. "It would be a great success, too—we could take up all the tickets—papa has great influence in the borough. Why do you not play in public here?"

"I content myself with a few pupils, at present."

"But you are so famous abroad—so——"

"Who told you?" asked Violet, quickly.

"A friend of mine—a gentleman who was here last night, and who said he had heard you both in Paris and Berlin."

"Yes, I have played in both cities, but I am

not famous. And I have given up seeking public applause. It bewilders me—I don't care for it," said Violet.

"Oh, how I should love it! Oh! to come up on a platform, and face a sea of heads, and be deafened by a roar of welcome—why, it would turn all the brains I have. And," she added, with a sudden, quaint humility, "I haven't many to boast of."

There was the first shade of something akin to regret on Fanny Oliver's countenance, but it quickly passed away, and she said, in a new, brisk tone—

"Do you like Birmingham?"

"I don't know," she replied. "I came here expecting to find a friend waiting for me, as she had promised."

"And was she not waiting?"

"Yes—in her coffin."

"Oh! how dreadful. What——"

Miss Hilderbrandt was too quick for her. She went on again—

"Hence I was quite alone, and had to make my own way, and my own friends. But

—yes, I like Birmingham—there is much kindness, much generous hospitality amongst you Warwickshire folk."

"You will stay in Birmingham some time, I hope?"

"Why?"

"I should like to be your friend," said Fanny, very earnestly. "And I think you would soon like me, if you tried."

"If I were going to remain, Miss Oliver, I would try, until you turned against me."

"Turned against——"

"But," she said, interrupting her again, "I am going away to-night."

"Not for good?"

"Yes, for good."

"Oh! it can't be—it shan't be!" cried Fanny Oliver, with new excitement. "Papa and mamma will not allow it. They are going to ask you to become my teacher—on your own terms—on any terms—papa will not mind."

"I have business of great importance that takes me away," said Violet, "and I must go."

"For how long?"

"I don't know. I cannot say it is probable that I shall ever return," was the reply.

"Oh! this is very dreadful," exclaimed Fanny. "Something will surely happen to alter your determination. I wanted you for a friend so badly. I haven't one real friend of my own to whom I can confide anything. Isn't that awful? Is it not deplorable?"

Violet was not quite certain that it was a matter for regret, so far as the real friend was concerned, and therefore answered a little evasively. To become the friend, confidante, and sister-confessor of this young lady scarcely seemed a light or enviable task, burdened as one would be, probably, by scores of little secrets.

"Look there," said Fanny, touching Violet's arm, "he's coming. Tell me what you think of him before he gets too close to hear us."

The window of Fanny's boudoir opened to the garden, where Marcus Dagnell, with a white silk handkerchief twisted several times round his neck for protection to his throat, was slowly promenading.

"That is Mr. Dagnell's brother, is it not?" asked Violet.

"Yes, *your* Mr. Dagnell's brother," said Fanny, with emphasis. "The elder brother, though. It is a great shame that knighthoods are not hereditary?"

"Does it matter?"

"It does to me," was the reply, "otherwise I should be Lady Dagnell some day. That would be a little compensation for——But what do you think of him?"

"I think of him?" repeated Violet.

"Is he as good-looking as his brother Tom?"

"He is scarcely as good-looking, I should say," said Violet, thus pressed for an opinion.

"He's a perfect fright," said Fanny, in a sepulchral whisper. "Did you ever see such a lemon complexion in your life?"

"I—I don't know. He is a little yellow this morning, but late hours are a sufficient reason for it."

"Not at all; he's always yellow. I believe his blood's yellow," said the dissatisfied Fanny, "and he's so dreadfully slow and stupid, it's unbearable at times," and here the spoiled girl stamped her foot petulantly on the soft carpet.

"But you are going to marry the gentleman," said Violet.

"I suppose it's all settled; papa wants me, and I have said 'Yes.' That's the fashionable way of putting it, is it not?"

"And you love him?" inquired Violet, becoming interested in her companion.

"I don't actually dislike him, always," was the reply. "And he is very fond of me,—at least, I imagine he is, though he never says so. But his family are respectably connected and wealthy, and papa has made a great big fortune, and I am an only child, and that's the story. Not a three-volume novel—but what do you think of it?"

Fanny Oliver looked boldly, almost defiantly, at Violet Hilderbrandt, who saw a new phase of character in the speaker—a something deeper and more womanly, perhaps, beneath the superficialities and frivolities with which Miss Oliver was heavily weighted.

"It is a story that will not end unhappily, unless——"

"Unless what?" asked Fanny, impetuously. "What were you going to say? Please tell me. You are clever and shrewd, and have seen a great deal of the world. I have been always *stuck* here, and know nothing—out of books. Unless what?"

"I was going to say unless he or you love anybody else," replied Violet. "It does not require a knowledge of the world then—and I am without all worldly knowledge, I am afraid —to guess that such a story will end most miserably."

"Such a story might—but this is an excellent match, everybody says. Excellent" and then Fanny Oliver began biting her lace handkerchief with a set of strong white teeth, and looking at her lover with eyes that were a trifle dim, until he advanced leisurely to the open window, and made his obeisance to the ladies.

CHAPTER XIII.

RECOMMENDING A FRIEND.

"IT'S a beautiful morning," said Marcus Dagnell, after a formal introduction to Miss Hilderbrandt, and some polite inquiries after the health of each lady. "I am taking a stroll in the garden in search of fresh air."

"I thought you did not care for fresh air?" said Fanny.

"Can't say I do, as a rule; but I'm dreadfully seedy this morning—knocked all to pieces, 'pon my honour."

"Papa has got a bad headache, too."

"Very likely," said Marcus, with unintentional but most crushing satire, "but I can't account for mine."

"How do you account for papa's?" said Fanny, very sharply.

Marcus paused at this inquiry. He was not prepared for so leading a question. It had not struck him that Mr. Oliver's ailment was in any way unaccountable till that instant, and then his gentlemanly instincts warned him he was on dangerous ground.

"Excitement about the soirée's going off well, and so on, I presume. But I haven't been excited myself," said Marcus. "I only took three or four glasses of champagne all the evening, and I did not dance much. Slitherwick had all the round dances with you, if you remember, so I could not have got giddy in that way. I am dreadfully giddy, though, with a red-hot six-pence kind of sensation in my chest, just there! Tom told me to take a brisk walk round the garden, and I am doing it as briskly as I can, but I don't like it. I always detested walking in a garden, round and round, like a mill-horse."

"We haven't your spacious park-land to luxuriate in," said Miss Oliver, floridly.

"You are very fortunate, I think, Fanny," said Marcus, "for, when a fellow dislikes gardens, a big one is worse than a little one. Are you not coming out this morning? This sort of thing all alone is dreadfully monotonous."

"Where's your brother?"

"Oh, he's writing a letter home in the library. Awful nonsense, because he has not been away twelve hours, and can't have anything to say."

"It must be a love-letter, then—I'm sure it must be a love-letter," said Fanny, springing up and clapping her hands. "Miss Hilderbrandt, let us have a peep at him through the library windows. Pray come, it will be such fun!"

"No, no," said Violet, shrinking from the suggestion, and with a horror of fun of any kind at that crisis of her life. "I will stroll in the garden, if you will, for a few moments, but I shouldn't like to disturb Mr. Dagnell."

"You might fire a cannon off in his ears, and not disturb him, Miss Hilderbrandt," said Marcus, "he's in what people call a 'brown study.'"

"It *must* be a love-letter," exclaimed Fanny again. "Now, Marcus, come here," she said, taking hold of the lappels of his morning coat, "is it not a love-letter? Is there not some fair, beautiful creature hidden away in Sussex, or in France somewhere, to whom your brother is writing? You know he is in love—who is the lady?"

"Upon my honour, Fanny, I—I—don't think Tom *is* in love with anybody," remarked Marcus, evidently embarrassed. "I never asked him, but I should say not."

"It must be some one abroad," said Fanny, with a doubtful glance at Violet Hilderbrandt again, "for it can't possibly be that old, disagreeable nipper of a cousin of yours—that would be too ridiculous. She's close on thirty, and wears glasses," she added, for Violet's further information, "so it's some one abroad. He hasn't had time since he has been in England to—— I'll go and ask him myself!"

"Here—I say, Fanny—look here—I wish you wouldn't, though," called Marcus after her, as she released her hold of his coat, and went at a swift rush out of the house and along the garden-path. But Fanny Oliver had no such intention in her mind as that which she had promulgated in order to alarm her lover. She was a little afraid of the younger brother, and though she had been his playfellow when a child, time had set him at a distance from her. She was contented with peeping in at him as he sat before Papa Oliver's desk in the library, writing a letter to his cousin, so that Ursula should not consider herself slighted in any way.

"There need be no secrets between us—another woman in your confidence, and 'poor me' in the cold!"

They were almost Ursula's parting words, and they rang their warning notes in his ears as he sat there puzzled what to say, even what to leave unsaid. It was almost his first letter to his cousin—it was certainly his first love-letter—and the task was far from easy. He had not been a great hand at "letter-writing" at any time—men fond of action and used to active lives seldom are—but here was a letter most difficult to indite, and growing a greater task the more he pondered over it. He felt already he could not tell Ursula everything, that Violet Hilderbrandt's secret was not his, much less Ursula's; that Violet Hilderbrandt had not trusted him with it even; and, after his journey to Birmingham, it was not a satisfactory confession to make to his cousin, that he knew not what was the particular form of danger by which Miss Hilderbrandt was menaced. Cousin Ursula would certainly not believe him, or would write him down an ass for still having faith in so mysterious and reticent a heroine. He had better indite a general epistle, stating that he had discovered the lady, who was a guest of the Olivers for the present, and that fuller particulars should arrive in the course of a few days. He would not say too much concerning her, and he would make a feature of the watch that had been set upon him from Littlehampton to Birmingham last night. That would assuredly interest Ursula, and prove it was a matter of grave consequence for which he had come down to Warwickshire; and as for the possible date of his return, oh,

that was impossible to decide until he had had
another conversation with Miss Hilderbrandt,
and so the less said about that the better, too.
All this settled in some fashion, or in an odd
fashion, and then the sheer necessity of putting
it in black and white, and in the pleasantest
form of caligraphy, as befitted a man writing
home to his sweetheart; ay, there was the
rub !

Tom Dagnell bit his pen hard, looked up at
the ceiling, and at the great bronze and ormolu
chandelier, the burners of which he carefully
counted, finally he stared out of window and
caught sight of Fanny Oliver peeping round
one of the panes.

" Good morning," he said, and "Good
morning," responded Fanny, not a little confused.

"Marcus said you were here," said Miss
Oliver, coming full front to the open window
now, "and sent me to ask if you were disposed
for a walk in the garden before luncheon,"—
which was a fib, but a graceful way of getting
out of a dilemma. "I didn't like to disturb

you, until I was sure you were not very, very busy."

"I have a letter to write—and a precious hard letter it is," said Tom, rubbing his hair the wrong way with his disengaged hand.

It can't be a love-letter, thought Fanny.

"Perhaps inspiration will come after a walk, Tom—may I be so bold as to call my future brother ' Tom ' again ?"

"Certainly you may. Why not ? Tom is my name."

"Miss Hilderbrandt is with us too," said Fanny.

"Is she ?" said Tom. " Then I think I *will* take a stroll round the grounds for half an hour."

He got up and joined the party, leaving all that was done of his letter—and that was the date and " My dear Ursula,"—written in a neat round hand on a sheet of note paper, upon the desk.

Yes, the fresh air was pleasant and refreshing after that stuffy library, and he was glad to be in it, shaking hands with Violet Hilderbrandt and congratulating her on her recovery from the fatigue of the preceding night. Miss Oliver, full of projects as well as spirits, was suddenly seized with an idea.

"Let us play lawn-tennis. Marcus plays, and here are the bats and balls. Why, we can have a delightful hour here; we are just the number."

Violet Hilderbrandt shook her head.

"I do not know the game," she answered.

"Ah, you wouldn't think much of it," said Marcus. "It's dreadfully tiring. I don't think much of it myself—it makes you jump so."

"Mr. Slitherwick plays beautifully, doesn't he?" said Fanny.

"Yes, it exactly suits him. He's a fellow that can jump. I've often thought he would have made a splendid linendraper."

"If you mean counter-jumper you had better say so, Marcus," said Fanny Oliver, severely.

"It's just the same," said Marcus.

"And Mr. Slitherwick is a friend of papa's— and of mine," added Fanny, with severe meaning.

"Exactly. That's why I wouldn't say a word against him for the world," said Marcus to Tom, " he's a splendid player at lawn-tennis. You should see him, Tom, it's a treat."

But Tom was not interested in the qualifications of Mr. Slitherwick for lawn-tennis; he dropped behind, took his place by the side of Miss Hilderbrandt, and went on slowly with her, leaving the engaged couple to themselves.

" I have been anxious to see you," murmured Violet, " I have been thinking of my next step very deeply."

" What do you propose doing ?"

" Leaving at once."

" That would be impolitic."

"I am not safe here. I must get away unperceived from the town, at any risk," said Violet, with her white brow furrowed.

"Patience, let me think a little for you presently, if you consider it imperative to go away."

" I do," she answered.

" Have you thought of any plan of action for yourself ?" he inquired.

"Hardly, I am still confused. I should be glad to get to Paris again, or to London, where perhaps my mother would join me," said Violet, thoughtfully. "Oh! if mother would come!"

"We will consider the position now. If I could be assured of the danger which is threatening you—if you could confide in me so far as that," urged Tom.

"I may tell you soon—very soon. Don't ask me to-day."

"Very well."

They had walked away from Marcus and Miss Oliver, and Fanny, watching them keenly at times, said,

"It's all nonsense, Marcus. Nothing will persuade me that they are not old friends—old lovers. Look at them."

"It is deuced like it," replied Marcus. "But he has never told me anything about the lady. Besides, there's the governor wouldn't have anything of that sort going on, and Ursula——"

"Oh! Ursula," exclaimed Fanny. "Now, Marcus, tell me about this Ursula, and what it all means, or I'll never speak to you again."

"Good gad, Fanny, what an awful threat!"

"Tom is not going to marry Ursula, is he?" she asked. "He has not been dragged into that?"

"I don't know much—but I'll tell you all I know, if you will not let it go any further," replied Marcus. "I can't bear having secrets from you; and, if Ursula told me not to say anything about her engagement to Tom, I am not bound to obey her commands, am I?"

"Certainly not, Marcus. Go on."

Marcus accordingly made a clean breast of the story of Tom's engagement, whilst Tom himself was drifting towards the same subject by degrees.

"I have been troubled very much this morning, Miss Hilderbrandt," he said, "—by a letter which I have to write, and in which I hardly know what to say about you."

"About me!" and she regarded Tom with surprise.

"I promised my cousin Ursula to send her all the news this morning—she read your telegram to me yesterday, and was—well, deeply interested in my journey and its object," said Tom.

"Your cousin Ursula," repeated Miss Hilderbrandt; "you might have spared me the risk of taking a third person into our confidence—for it is a great risk."

"Not in this instance," he replied. "She is the most unselfish, the most honourable of women."

"Is she at Broadlands ?"

"Yes. My father was her guardian after the death of his brother—she has been with us many years."

"Many years! More than five ?" asked Violet, wonderingly.

"Oh, yes; fifteen perhaps."

"But your home was unhappy. You were treated with so much injustice that you fled from it," said Violet, remembering the faint outline of his history, which he had sketched for her on board ship last March.

"Yes, exactly; but I did not understand her then," said Tom. "She was a mystery to me; she had taken great pains to conceal her true nature from us all, and I was not watchful or considerate. I—I almost hated her before I came home."

"How strangely you must have been deceived," remarked Violet.

"I never did understand women, I suppose," said Tom; "and, at all events, she was an enigma to me. But I returned to find I had cruelly misjudged her—that she had been all her life my friend—the friend of all of us. She had sacrificed her whole fortune—a large fortune even—to save my father from a sudden ruin— even a public disgrace—which was impending over him. And it was on one condition—that I should return to Broadlands and be reinstated in my place—and that my father should ask forgiveness of me for all his past injustice. There—that is the end of the story I told you on *The Witch*. I never speak of it to her, she will not listen; but you may guess what a good woman she is, and how terribly I had misunderstood her in the dark old days."

Violet Hilderbrandt forgot her own history in that of Tom Dagnell. She proceeded very thoughtfully by his side, with her dark eyes bent upon the gravel path.

"Is that the end of the story?" she asked, "the very end?"

"We are engaged to be married. *That* is the end," answered Tom.

"I thought so. It is how all pleasant stories should end," said Violet Hilderbrandt, with a little sigh. "Yes, she must have loved you very much indeed."

"She had rendered herself penniless for my sake—she had acted nobly and unselfishly, far more than I can explain, or you would care to hear, and—and—I asked her to be my wife."

"Loving her very much, too?"

"Yes,—of course."

"Of course," repeated Violet Hilderbrandt. "But—may I ask why you tell me all this, why you confide in one who keeps her own revelations so completely in the background?"

"I wish you to be interested in her very deeply, to understand that hers is no common mind, or common heart—to write to her even, and tell her your whole history, so that she may be one more true friend to you," said Tom.

"Could I trust one of my own sex more quickly than I could trust you?" said Violet; "no, I think not. And yet," she added, hesitatingly, "this lady must be far above us all—a true-hearted, generous, and unselfish woman."

"She is shrewd and far-seeing also—and—"

"And—jealous of your coming to my rescue?" added Violet.

Tom drew a quick breath at this—it was so close to the truth.

"All women are jealous, more or less, and Ursula is a woman, not a goddess," Tom confessed. "Yes, she was a little jealous last night, until I reasoned with her and promised her the whole story to-day. I did not think— it did not strike me—that you would not tell me anything."

Violet Hilderbrandt walked on in silence for a few minutes after this. She was troubled, but there was a new, strange light flickering on her face, a new hope springing up within her heart.

"She must be a brave, strong woman," she said, at last. "I will see her to-night, Mr. Dagnell, and tell her all!"

CHAPTER XIV.

TOM'S LETTER.

TOM DAGNELL was surprised and gratified at the announcement which Violet Hilderbrandt had made to him. It was approaching the end; the mystery which surrounded her, and against which he had protested, was rapidly drifting away!

"Yes, I will tell your cousin my history," Violet continued, "she will not judge me too quickly, or disbelieve me too soon. Such women as Ursula are very scarce, Mr. Dagnell. I shall be glad to see her—it is advice like hers that I shall profit by."

"Ye-es," said Tom, with a faint degree of hesitation visible in him, for the first time, at this exhibition of Violet's enthusiasm, "she will be a good friend. She is shrewd enough, but her advice may not be, after all, the best for you."

"Why not?" asked Violet, wonderingly.

"She is impulsive," was the reply, "and I am not quite certain she is particularly wise. She sacrificed her whole fortune for one idea— and she accepted me as her future husband for another. Clearer-headed women would have hesitated a little longer in both these matters."

"She is unselfish and truthful, that is sufficient. She has known trouble too, and will understand me," said Violet.

"You may trust her with your life," said Tom, warmly, "she is more of a heroine than a woman; but her advice may not be sound. She has no knowledge of the world."

"It is all the better for her judgment upon me that she should not have any," answered Violet, quietly, "she will believe me more completely."

"Very good," said Tom.

" And now will you kindly take me to Broadlands, and introduce me to her? I will not
detain her very long," said Violet. " Let us
get away from Birmingham, at once—I am sure
I may ask this favour of you?"

" You may ask any favour of me in the world,
Miss Hilderbrandt," Tom said, " and I shall be
only too glad to help you. But we must not
act too precipitately. Yours is a case that requires more than ordinary time for reflection."

" What do you suggest?" she asked,
anxiously.

" Extreme caution, if you would leave Birmingham unwatched," said Tom. " It will be
difficult to quit the town to-day unperceived,
and with your father and his spies on the alert;
and, granted that we are successful in eluding
their vigilance, there would be a deal of curiosity aroused in this establishment at our
sudden departure together."

" I will go alone," said Violet.

" You will be seen, and you will be suspected," Tom replied.

" Ah! yes.. I am hemmed in, and defenceless. Tell me what you think is the better plan,. then—you are wiser than I," she said.

"To write to Ursula, and await her arrival," replied Tom. "Till then not to trouble ourselves in any way, feeling we are safe, and amongst friends."

" *We !* You talk as if you were sharing my suspense."

"I am," answered Tom, warmly.

"Thank you," was the grateful response, " but that is as impossible as sharing the consequence. Impossible, as—but there," she said, checking herself, " I will be guided by your advice—I will wait. It is not evident that Miss Dagnell will care for my confession. She may doubt me all the more for offering to confide in her. When do you write?"

"Immediately."

" You will state everything clearly?"

" Everything I know," was the dry answer.

" Ah, don't satirize me, please," said Miss Hilderbrandt, in a tone so piteous that Tom's heart smote him. "I—I—am learning to understand you very quickly, and you must forgive me if I wish to tell your cousin, first of all. She, who has faith in you that will last her life, will advise me what to do—will know whether I dare ask your further help. I will, if you will allow me, write a few lines to be enclosed in your letter to her."

"Yes, yes," replied Tom, bewildered by this exhibition of sudden confidence in Ursula Dagnell, "it will be wise—it will pave the way for the meeting to follow."

"You think I do not trust you, Mr. Dagnell," said Violet, with a sad smile, "and yet I take your cousin's virtues at your word, and will keep nothing from her."

"It will please Ursula very much to be the first recipient of your confidence," answered Tom, but in his heart he was not quite so sure of this—the whole position was not quite so clear as he could wish it to be. There were two Ursulas before him, and they were at variance with each other. The fretful Ursula of yesterday hurling at him and Violet her jealous invectives, and the woman who had saved the house of Dagnell from ruin and disgrace, were hardly to be assimilated, save by that strong love for him which had rendered her both just and unjust.

He returned to the library at Violet's request to finish his letter, to state the whole facts of the case, and the new light which Miss Hilderbrandt had thrown upon them by her determination to confide in Ursula; but the statement, after all, was not particularly clear, and he found himself floundering and blundering still amidst his explanations. No, it was not a clear story to commit to black and white, and the man, who hated mystery, felt that he was concocting a most mysterious and unsatisfactory epistle. If he could have told his story to Ursula it would have been an infinitely better plan—the art of narrating it was almost beyond him. He had to interest his cousin, to the best of his power, in Miss Hilderbrandt, and in her misfortunes, whatever they might be; and he was not quite certain that his description of her and her sorrows would be completely acceptable to Ursula, eloquent as he had grown in the cause which he was pleading, and strong as were his convictions in the injustice by which Miss Hilderbrandt was oppressed. He read and re-read the letter which he had indited, and groaned over its want of perspicuity; he had endeavoured to arouse·Ursula's interest, and even enthusiasm, but he felt that his composition was hardly likely to prove a success. He had given Ursula Dagnell "a good character" to Violet Hilderbrandt, and he had been believed at once implicitly, but he doubted if reversing the compliment would be equally as successful at Broadlands. When the two women faced each other that would be a very different thing, for the truth and candour of each would be quickly apparent, but this confounded pen and ink sketch was an uphill task. It was, however, a mere preliminary. Violet entered the library at his signal, to add those few words of her own which would make matters clear, and interest Ursula in her new friend; and he was surprised once more at the rapidity with which she dashed off a missive to one whom she had never seen.

"Will that do?" she said, passing the note across to Tom.

Tom took it from her and perused it.

"I am anxious to trust in you and tell you all the truth," she wrote. "I have said nothing to your cousin. I need a brave woman's sympathy, and that you are brave and true I am assured. Let me come to Broadlands as quickly as possible, and go away strengthened by your counsel."

"Yes, that will do," said Tom, thoughtfully.

She had set Ursula Dagnell down as a wise woman, after all, thought Tom; he almost wished he had spoken less in favour of his cousin. He could not tell why—he had hardly been prepared for the exhibition of so much confidence in his statement—he had been anxious to console Ursula as well as Violet Hilderbrandt—he had painted to Violet the picture of his heroine in glowing colours, and as he only saw it for himself, and as no one else had seen it for a single instant. He was not satisfied; it was all true enough, but he could almost imagine that he was on the verge of another mistake, so suddenly had followed a revulsion of the feeling which had prompted him to press Ursula's friendship upon the bewildered girl.

"That will do," he said again. Then after a moment's further hesitation, which Violet did not perceive, he closed the letter and fastened it.

"She will judge us fairly——she will be Violet Hilderbrandt's friend," he muttered to himself, as he dropped the letter in the box on Mr. Oliver's table, where it would remain till the servant came to clear it for the next despatch from Birmingham.

CHAPTER XV.

HAVING made up their minds to a state of rest—to a patient waiting for results—Tom and Violet seemed to settle down. In a few hours they were almost at home at Elmslie House, and the mystery about them appeared to recede into the background amongst the common-places of everyday life by which they were surrounded. Tom sent a groom to the "Hen and Chickens" for his portmanteau, with explanations and apologies, and found that it had been delivered last night and no inquiries made concerning it afterwards. Violet Hilderbrandt's luggage was already at the railway-station, packed and ready for departure. She had been prepared twenty-four hours since, she said—and now there was time before them to reflect, to wait, to hope!

They were quickly at their ease in the manufacturer's vast establishment, where there was no stint of Birmingham hospitality or warmth of welcome.

Miss Oliver took credit to herself for persuading Violet Hilderbrandt to remain a day or two at Elmslie House; and her pleasure was evinced by many little extravagances of demeanour to which there is no occasion to direct our reader's attention. Here was the one friend, the one *confidante*, the one after her own heart, Fanny Oliver thought and even said, and, at least, it was satisfactory to Violet Hilderbrandt to feel that she was not regarded in any way as an intruder in the household.

"One must soon like these Olivers, despite their little vanities," said Tom to her later in the day. "They are anxious to please, and to see us pleased. Are you reconciled to the position?"

"I have found the courage to wait," she answered. "I feel stronger—I am not alone," she added, after a moment's pause.

"Thank you for the compliment, Miss Hilderbrandt, I take that to myself," he said.

"It was intended for you, but not for a compliment," answered Violet, "and it shows what a selfish coward I am. For, after all," she added, thoughtfully regarding him, "I have brought you a long journey in vain."

"Not in vain," answered Tom. "You have come here at my wish, and you are safer here than in Bath Row. I am at your side to be of service, if there is any danger."

"If!" she repeated. "Ah! perhaps this is all a dream. My father told you I was mad, and the slave of delusions."

"We will talk no more of the old subject, please," cried Tom. "I am your physician, and interdict it. Cannot you set it aside?"

"I will try," she replied. "I have studied to deceive myself and others before this. Not always with success though," she added, with a sigh.

"It was not likely."

"I thought on board *The Witch*, from something which you said to me, that your home had been like mine; but, after all, yours has been a happy life, in comparison," she added, "and I was very much mistaken. I am glad of that."

"My home was awfully unhappy, once," he said.

"And yet Ursula Dagnell was there!"

She did not make home happy—rather, she had added to the misery and distrust there—but Tom did not re-assert this. He had spoken too highly of Ursula Dagnell that morning to inveigh against his bitter past again.

"Yes, she was there," he said in reply.

"But as for me! Why, this is my first experience of a home—of anything that approaches to my idea of what a home should be," she said, enthusiastically. "I live for the first time amongst natural and rational human beings. I am happier, breathing the same air with them— all this is a new, bright, innocent world to me. I have known no home before!"

Her cheeks flushed and her eyes brightened and dilated as she spoke. What a little it would take to make this poor hunted girl content, Tom thought, if the clouds were once dispelled about her life. What a past hers had been in some dark, desperate way—and how different from his own! Surely, it was easy to change it all now?

It was not an unpleasant day at Elmslie House, when all thoughts of the uncertain future were set aside at last, as Tom Dagnell had recommended that they should be. It was wise to live in the present; sufficient for to-morrow was the evil thereof; here was one day to be marked with a white stone. There was peace—even happiness—for these two, in looking back at it, presently; it was an episode in both their lives; the resting-place on the rock before the tide rolled in upon them once more.

The warm-hearted and wealthy Warwickshire folk were proud of their guests, and there was no patronage in the midst of their display. They were rich—had got rich within the last few years, and were hardly used to it; for they liked the world to see how well off they were, and were obliged when anybody respected them for it.

Tom felt that Mr. Oliver and his wife improved upon further acquaintance, though it was hard work to admire everything—pictures, old china, buhl-work, and plate, and Mr. Oliver was eager to show everything, and to whisper confidentially in Tom's ear the exact sum he had given for each article. When the resources of the establishment had been exhibited, Mr. Oliver was more at his ease and more natural ; he could be eloquent in his rough style on the subject matter of his collections, on names and dates of his "antiquities" ; and as for his own business, he had mastered it completely, and was the commander of a thousand men.

"You must inspect the factory before you go, Mr. Tom," said Mr. Oliver. "I shall take it as an unfriendly act if you leave Birmingham without seeing the works, mind."

This was after dinner, before the ladies had withdrawn from the dessert. It had been a grand dinner in its way, and two of the choicest pines had been cut for dessert from the glass-house in the rear of the premises.

"I shall be glad to see the works," said Tom.

"And Miss Hilderbrandt will allow me the honour to escort her?" said Mr. Oliver, with a profound bow.

"If I have time," replied Violet, "I will come. I shall be pleased to come."

"You will like the show-room, too. It's quite a drawing-room. You may as well all come, and Marcus can bring Fanny again."

"Tha-anks," said Marcus, "very much, but I really had such a splitting headache last time, with all that horrid machinery buzzing and rattling about, that I must ask you to excuse me."

"All right, Marcus—you are your own master here. Once is enough, perhaps, to see the old mill where the grist comes in," said Mr. Oliver, somewhat crestfallen.

"Quite enough," asserted Marcus. "It's an awfully interesting place, Tom, but you'll find half an hour of it about as much as any man can stand who hasn't a soul, as it were, for dish-covers. But it's awfully interesting."

"Yes, and we'll make up a party and go," said Fanny, very decisively. "I like the factory, and I mean you to like it too, Marcus."

"I do like it," murmured Marcus, "but the noise hardly agrees with my head, that's all."

"And that's all we want to hear about your head to-night, Marcus, please," said Fanny, very pertly, "and I hope it will be strong enough to endure the music after dinner. We shall have—oh! we shall have—a little music this evening," added Miss Oliver, looking across at Violet, and clasping her jewelled fingers together. "You will favour us, Miss Hilderbrandt? You are looking so well to-night that Mr. Tom will not even call us brutes for asking you to play."

"That's one for both of you boys, that is," roared forth Mr. Oliver, hammering the table with the handle of his dessert-knife; "we can hold our own against the aristocracy of Littlehampton, now and then. Bravo, Fanny—give it them again!"

"Did I say 'brutes'?" inquired Tom. "I was excited; I am afraid I was very rude last night."

"Well, you were a little bit," confessed Mr. Oliver; "but, Lor' bless you, we thought nothing of it. Slitherwick might have been put out a trifle, for he went away without saying good night, after you had shoved him in the stomach, but he's a good fellow, and soon comes round. He's worth his fifty thou., is Slitherwick. Try another glass of that port, Master Tom; it's the real thing—24 port—and you may guess what that cost. Twenty-four, sir, Marco," pushing the decanter towards him; "one more glass."

"Tha-anks," said Marcus, passing the decanter on to his brother, "I daren't touch any more of it. I prefer a decent claret to twenty-four shilling port even—I mean eighteen twenty-four port. God bless me, I am rather absent this evening."

"You are," said Fanny, meaningly, again.

"I can't help it. I have really a bad head-ache, Fanny," he said, anxious for the consola-

tion of her sympathy, "and we kept it up terribly late last night.   In Littlehampton we consider 11 p.m. a late hour."

"I would not live in such a dull hole for the
world," said Fanny, with great decision.

"It is rather dull, but it's not a hole exactly,"
answered Marcus.

"You may like it, but I couldn't bear it."

"I have lived there all my life—so has Tom,"
said Marcus.

"No, he ran away from it," answered Fanny,
who had evidently made up her mind to be
contradictory that evening, "he could not bear
it either, once upon a time,—could you, Tom?"

It was not a pleasant subject to discuss, and
the remembrance of the old quarrel was still
acute and painful, but Tom did not testify any
embarrassment.

"No, I could not bear it once," he said, easily,
but there was something in Tom's looks that
brought the talk to a standstill.   Presently Mrs.
Oliver rose, and the ladies followed her into the
drawing-room, and within a quarter of an hour
the gentlemen made their appearance, despite

a slight reluctance on Mr. Oliver's part to leave his "24 port."

The drawing-room at Elmslie House had once more assumed its general aspect; it had been the ball-room of a few hours since, but plenty of hands had been at work all day, and the costly furniture was in its place, bright and new enough even for Lady Dagnell's tastes, thought our hero.

" You will play to us?" said Fanny, entreatingly, to Violet, " oh! I hope you are well enough to play to-night."

" I will play with pleasure," Violet answered.

She had scarcely sat down to the grand piano when Mr. Slitherwick entered unannounced, very much like the friend of the family that he was, and made a few inquiries as to the health of the Olivers, and even of the Dagnells, and was honoured with that formal introduction to Miss Hilderbrandt with which he had not been favoured the preceding evening.

" Is Slitherwick always here?" asked Tom of his brother.

"Pretty nearly," replied Marcus; "he is not a bad sort when you know him thoroughly."

" Ah, I never shall know him thoroughly," said Tom.

" Don't you like him?" asked Marcus, curiously.

" I have no feeling in the matter. Do *you* like him here so often?" was the rejoinder.

" Well, hardly," said the elder brother. "It doesn't much matter to me, of course, but I don't care about it. He is——"

" Shut up, Marcus. Miss Hilderbrandt has begun to play."

" That's no reason why I should shut up," said Marcus, " for——"

" And I want to listen, old boy," said Tom, interrupting him again. " Miss Hilderbrandt's playing is not like anybody else's—it's perfection."

" Miss Hilderbrandt is not like anyone else either," whispered Marcus, " for she's perfection too, in my worthy brother's estimation, or I am deucedly mistaken."

Tom stared at Marcus.

"You are sharp this evening," he said, in a low tone.

"'Pon my honour, I am not," replied his brother. "You have heard me say my head aches, and I am a trifle confused. But still I am not blind, and if you'll follow my advice——"

"Well?" said Tom, as Marcus paused.

"The less you say of all this to Ursula the better."

"Why?"

"Ursula is not a woman to take anything very calmly; at least, anything in this way," Marcus replied. "That's my opinion, of course, but I fancy, if I were you, I wouldn't say too much about Miss Hilderbrandt to Ursula. I wouldn't, indeed."

"I have no secrets from Ursula. There is nothing to keep back."

"Hush, hush, gentlemen!" cried Mr. Slitherwick, in mild protest at the brothers' muttered conversation, and Tom felt angry with himself and everybody else at having been called to order by the gunmaker. It showed that he was inattentive and indifferent to Miss Hilderbrandt's playing, and this was not the case, only Marcus had been particularly aggravating in his unconscious way. And as for the gunmaker, well, Tom would have been glad to punch his head for his intolerable officiousness. Slitherwick wished Violet to see he was interested in her performance, and that he would not, if possible, lose a single note of it—a very polite sort of fellow, this Slitherwick. Tom forgot the gunmaker in a few minutes, however—the spell of the wondrous music was upon him again; here were genius and power, and a perfect command of the instrument. It was no wonder that Mr. Hilderbrandt was anxious for the return of his daughter; there was a fortune in her, and in the engagements he could make for her.

"I heard you play that at Berlin, Miss Hilderbrandt," observed Mr. Slitherwick when she had concluded. "I went three nights consecutively to hear you."

"You are fond of music?" she inquired.

"I am passionately devoted to music."

"Do you play?"

"Oh! yes," said Slitherwick, "I have studied under half a dozen masters."

"You will favour us, perhaps?" said Violet.

"Certainly, with pleasure," and the bold Slitherwick, unabashed at the contrast, sat down on the music-stool which Violet Hilderbrandt had vacated, and poured forth the little soul that was in him. It was very indifferent melody after Miss Hilderbrandt's, and there did not seem much time or a great deal of tune in it, but the gentleman strummed on complacently, with Fanny Oliver, at least, for a patient listener, and with Marcus making wry faces under the infliction.

"I suppose we may talk now?" Marcus muttered to Tom, who made no reply, but continued to stare at the window at the extremity of the room. A few minutes afterwards, Tom Dagnell turned to Violet.

"Do you know this piece?" he asked, in a cool and unconcerned manner.

"Yes."

" Is there much more of it ?"

" Yes, plenty more," said Violet, with her old bright smile suddenly apparent at his question.

" Let us stroll into the conservatory," he murmured—" I should like to talk to you for a few minutes."

The smile disappeared, and Violet looked at him steadily; he was calm and grave, but there had come a change to him.

" I would prefer to remain—unless——"

" Unless I have anything important to communicate," he said. " Well, don't look astonished, or let them see you are. I have !"

" Tell me what it is. I can be very cool and self-possessed. I have been trained in a good school for it. Something *has* happened ? "

" Yes."

" Lately ?—within the last few minutes, do you mean ?" she inquired.

" Yes," he responded, with a glance at the window again. " Pass into the conservatory, and I will follow you."

"No; I understand you. I am quite prepared," said Violet, very firmly. "We are found out—we are watched?"

"Yes," said Tom Dagnell, for the third time, "we are watched."

CHAPTER XVI.

THE MESSAGE.

VIOLET HILDERBRANDT was not to be readily dismayed that evening. Put on her guard by Tom, she was quick to comprehend the position, and to act up to it. A slight flickering of the colour in her cheeks, a glance towards the uncurtained windows at the end of the drawing-room, and then she was apparently at her ease. She turned a little aside from the guests, and leaned over a table upon which were several drawing-room volumes, one of which she opened, as though interested in its steel engravings. Her small white hand might have shaken for an instant, but there was no one save Tom to perceive it.

"What can I do?" asked Tom. "I am here to obey all commands."

"Who watches us? My father?"

"No; a boy who was at New-street Station yesterday, and who was with your father in the cab that followed mine," replied Tom. "He has been peering through that window once or twice. I knew the face at once. Don't look; he is there again."

"You are sure he was with my father?"

"Yes."

"He brings a message from him, then. See to him, please, for me."

"But——"

Violet Hilderbrandt had closed the book, rose, and crossed to the piano, where she appeared to be deeply interested in the Slitherwick blunders on that much afflicted instrument. She had wished to put an end to any further dialogue between Tom and herself, but the old fear of discovery had left her, or else the event having come, and all efforts to elude observation having failed most miserably, she was prepared for the worst. How was it that Mr.

Hilderbrandt had sent a message to her? and why, having found the daughter of whom he had been in search, did not Mr. Hilderbrandt come himself to claim her, as he had been anxious to do at Littlehampton?

Tom did not reflect upon this any great while; the dark eyes of Miss Hilderbrandt were upon him; the business of his life, the mystery of hers, had begun again before the night was ended. He rose and strolled leisurely into the conservatory without anyone being aware of his departure; at the extremity of the conservatory there was a door opening into the garden, and this he unlocked cautiously, closed after him, and went along the garden side of the house towards the place where he had perceived the spy, and where he found him curled up on a rustic garden-seat as though he had expected to be attended to presently.

Tom approached the lad. Yes, it was the ragged, bare-footed, shock-headed youth of last night, who glared up at him, and whose white, wan face was singularly distinct in the star-light. Tom noticed also that, at some earlier period of life, the boy's nose had been broken and badly set.

"I thought you'd seed me," said the lad in a husky voice, "I held up my hand twice. Yer nodded back, didn't yer?"

"Yes, Larry," said Tom, "I did."

"How d' yer know my name's Larry?" asked the boy, surprised in his turn.

"Your master called you so last night, when you followed in the cab."

"Yes, that was a lark, and yer got the best on us too when yer cleared the blooming fence," said Larry, "but the guv'nor spotted yer this morning; he's not easily done, the old un, is he?"

"Not easily," replied Tom, coolly; "now, what do you want?"

"I've brought a message to the gal."

"From the governor?" asked Tom.

"That's it."

"Hand it over."

The boy fumbled about the ragged fringe of his left pocket, and produced a small sealed note, which he placed in Tom Dagnell's hands.

It was a business-like transaction, carried out without any display on either side; Tom having resolved to be as self-possessed as any of them. Surprise or confusion should not betray that he was off his guard, and the messenger was not in any way struck by his demeanour, but, on the contrary, probably thought it natural under the circumstances.

"Is this all?" said Tom.

"Yes, that's all," said Larry. "But don't keep a cove long about the ans'er. It's none too warm here, I can tell yer."

"Oh, you are waiting for an answer?"

"Yes,—and I say, old un!"

"Well—young un."

"What have yer done with the dog—he ain't about, is he?"

"No."

"It'll be the worse for him, if he is. *I* ain't a-going to stand any more of his larks," said Larry, decisively.

"What will you do, if any of the servants find you here?" said Tom.

"Oh, no fear. Leave that to Larry. Don't

yer trouble abont him," said the youth, con-
ceitedly.

"Very well."

Tom walked slowly back to the house, with
the letter in the breast-pocket of his coat. The
ease and assurance of the boy who had brought
the message puzzled him a great deal; the connection between Larry and Mr. Hilderbrandt
was difficult to guess at, although a strange suspicion was gathering force within Tom's mind.
He returned to the house and passed from
the conservatory into the drawing-room; Mr.
Slitherwick's rhapsody on the piano had reached a termination, and he was discoursing upon
the music of the future with Miss Hilderbrandt,
who had been drawn into an argument with
him, and was refuting quietly a few of his
propositions. Fanny Oliver was listening, and
endeavouring to understand it all; Mr. and
Mrs. Oliver were listening also, but making no
attempt to understand; Marcus Dagnell sat
bolt upright in his chair, with his eyes closed in
slumber.

"You are fond of plants, Master Tom?" said Mr. Oliver, as he entered.

"Yes. I have been glancing at your collection."

"I believe they are very fine. I don't know anything about them myself. I pay a big bill for them every month, and that's my part of the transaction," said Mr. Oliver.

Tom sat down once more at the table, and it was not long before Miss Hilderbrandt broke away from the bonds of argument, and came back to her old place near him. The position had changed then; Fanny Oliver was beginning to sing, and Mr. Slitherwick to turn over the leaves of her music; Marcus, who had suddenly opened his eyes, was looking dreamily at them both; Mr. and Mrs. Oliver were talking together over a little tea-table, at which the latter had presided after dinner.

"There is the message which you expected," said Tom, passing the letter to Violet at the first opportunity.

"Expected!" she repeated. "Oh! yes."

"The bearer waits an answer," added Tom.

"Yes, yes, presently," she murmured. "If I had only followed my own impulse, and gone away this morning, here was one trial from which I might have been spared."

"I did not think they would have discovered us so speedily," said Tom. "I am very sorry; it is all my fault. Tell me what next I can do, or what is to be done?"

"One moment," she replied. "I will return in one moment, after I have read this."

She passed out of the drawing-room, and Tom opened the door for her, closed it behind her, and returned to his seat to find that Marcus had taken the chair which Miss Hilderbrandt had vacated.

Fanny Oliver, at a very high pitch indeed, was screaming "The Power of Love," when Marcus said,

"Miss Hilderbrandt can't bear Fanny's singing, I suppose, Tom? That's one drawback to Fanny—her high notes are simply dreadful."

"I don't know—I cannot say," answered Tom, irrelevantly.

"It is no business of mine to interfere, Tom:

and of course you know best what *is* best;
but if there's not something like an understand-
ing between you and Miss Hilderbrandt, I am
very much mistaken. And—it is not quite fair
to Ursula, in my small opinion, that's all," concluded Marcus.

"Unfortunately, Marcus, there is no under-
standing between me and Miss Hilderbrandt,"
replied Tom, savagely. "Only an infernal thick
cloud into which she disappears, leaving nothing
tangible in her stead."

"Good gad! you talk like Ixion."

"No, I talk like a fool!" muttered Tom.

"That's about the same thing, for—what's
the matter now?"

Tom's hand had fallen on Marcus's arm, and
gripped it hard; and Tom's face had changed
colour, despite the self-command of which he
was somewhat vain. The younger brother looked round cautiously. Miss Oliver was warbling
on complacently; Mr. Slitherwick was bending
over her and the music, Oliver *père* and *mère*
were still chatting unconcernedly, and Oliver
père was counting something on his fingers,

probably the expense of the preceding night's
festivity. It was only Tom Dagnell's quick
ears that had heard light feet pass along the
hall without, and the street door close the instant afterwards.

"GONE!" he whispered to himself.

CHAPTER XVII.

LARRY.

MARCUS DAGNELL removed his arm from his brother's grip, and rubbed the place assaulted very carefully.

"Upon my honour, I don't make you out, to-night," he muttered. "Is it the port that Old Oliver's so proud of?"

"I'm not drunk," said Tom, sternly.

".What do you mean by 'gone'? Miss Hilderbrandt hasn't——"

"I cannot be worried by your questions, Marcus," said Tom.

He rose and went out of the room with rapid strides, unconsciously slamming the door behind him with a force that frightened Mrs. Oliver into her tea-tray, and caused a sudden stoppage in the "Power of Love."

"That's the rudest young cub we have ever had in this house," growled Mr. Oliver to his wife. "Foreign politeness, I suppose—for I'm hanged if it's English."

"If he did not care to hear Fanny sing, he need not have made such a noise running away," said Mrs. Oliver in feeble protest, "but, perhaps, the door slipped."

"Slipped be damned!" growled Mr. Oliver, "he did it on purpose. He's been walking all over the house ever since he has left the dinner-table—in and out—in and out, like a wild beast, —and Miss Hilderbrandt might have waited until Fanny had finished, I should think. Here he is again!"

Yes, Tom Dagnell had re-appeared, following the footman who had brought in a little note upon a salver for Miss Oliver. Curiosity had led him back in this instance, and with his hat on, which he had forgotten to remove. The note was from Violet to Fanny, he was certain.

"Oh, how tiresome; how strange!" said

Fanny, as she perused two lines hastily written in lead pencil; "a friend wishes to see Miss Hilderbrandt at once, on business of importance —she can't wait a minute, she will explain when she returns, she says."

"She will return, then?" muttered Tom, as he left the room precipitately once more.

"There he goes again," said Mr. Oliver; "I don't believe he *is* quite right, mind you."

"Oh, good gracious!" replied his wife, "don't say that, Jonathan, you make me quite nervous to think of it."

"It is my own impression that he and that foreign girl are awful sick of us, and have gone for a walk down the Hagley-road to get out of Fanny's row," said Mr. Oliver, and, having promulgated this theory, he suggested billiards to Marcus and Slitherwick.

Marcus had no particular objection, but Slitherwick was pressed for time, and had only ten more minutes to spare, an announcement which made Marcus waver in his intention, until Mr. Oliver pinioned him and led him off arm-in-arm.

"Come along, Marcus, we'll give them the slip, too, as it's all in the fashion this evening," he said, as they went along the corridor towards the billiard-room.

"Ye—es, exactly. There seems an unaccountable deal of running about, I fancy," replied Marcus.

"Elmslie Lunatic Asylum would be more appropriate than Elmslie House," said Mr. Oliver. "The way people behave in it just now is very remarkable to me. Is your brother Tom always so eccentric?"

"He may be a trifle eccentric, now and then," responded Marcus; "you never exactly know what he is going to do next."

"In the family, sir—depend upon it."

"Good gad!"

"When your father was a young man—and we were a couple of city sprigs together—he wasn't all there, you know."

"Where was the rest of him?" asked Marcus. "I don't see——"

"He wasn't quite the thing here," said Mr. Oliver, tapping his own broad forehead. "He was a dull, heavy sort of fellow—something of your style, unless he was put out, and then Mount Vesuvius all ablaze was nothing to him."

"And that's something in Tom's style, too. Our failings are purely hereditary, I have no doubt," observed Marcus, "but we will not say anything more about them this evening. I would prefer not, if you will so far oblige me, Mr. Oliver."

"Certainly, my boy, certainly," said Mr. Oliver in reply, as Marcus fixed him with a glassy stare. "No offence, of course?"

"Oh! no. I always endeavour to avoid taking offence," replied Marcus. "It brings on a bad play of facial muscles, I have observed; it's as bad as laughing to me."

"Is it?" said Mr. Oliver.

"And I never laugh, if I can possibly help it."

"So I have perceived," was Mr. Oliver's answer.

They began billiards after this, each playing in a business-like fashion, and without comment on the game. Mr. Oliver lighted a cigar, and offered his case to Marcus, who said, "Tha-anks," but declined smoking; the servant brought in brandy and seltzer, and retired again; finally Mr. Slitherwick, a good hour and a half afterwards, dropped in to say "good night," and put Mr. Oliver out in a crack stroke.

"Your brother has not returned," he said to Marcus, "I thought possibly he might be with you."

"He's not here," said Marcus, after which piece of unnecessary information he went on with his game.

"I should have gone off the red easily, if you had not come in with a bang, Slitherwick," grumbled Mr. Oliver, as Marcus seized his advantage and began to score heavily.

Mr. Slitherwick apologised. He had entered in a great hurry; he had had no idea how the time had slipped away in the drawing-room until he had suddenly looked at his watch, and then he actually felt that he must make a run for it.

"Ah! well, look here," said Mr. Oliver, who was scarcely as amiable as usual that evening;

"don't make another run for it, till I have made this stroke, at any rate. It's my turn now—and I ought to do it."

"It requires the finest touch," said Mr. Slitherwick, shutting one eye to admire the position of the balls, "one of your very best touches, Mr. Oliver."

"Yes, but I'm not at my best to-night, I am afraid."

The stroke required was difficult, and put Mr. Oliver into a difficult, even a complicated and contorted position, with his cue twisted under his left arm, his body inclined forwards at a perilous angle, his eyes protruding, and his tongue out. Marcus and Mr. Slitherwick waited breathlessly for the stroke; it was a moment, two or three moments, of intense interest, the bronze clock on the mantel-piece was heard ticking very loudly amidst the silence; but the stroke never came, the balls were quiescent on the green cloth, and the cue remained motionless behind Mr. Oliver's back and under his left arm. Marcus and Slitherwick slowly raised their eyes from the table to regard Mr.

Oliver with faint surprise at the delay, and then with astonishment at his changed aspect. Mr. Oliver was not preparing for his stroke. He was glaring straight ahead of him.

"Good gracious! What's the matter?" said Slitherwick.

"It looks like a fit to me," said Marcus, coolly.

But it was no fit. Mr. Oliver was only "fixed" with amazement and fright, until the cue fell to the floor, and he pointed to the window of the billiard-room.

"There's somebody in the garden! Somebody looked in at the window, just this moment. Collar him, Marcus; collar him! We've had lots of robberies about here lately, and— why the devil don't you run, somebody?"

It was Mr. Slitherwick who dashed courageously into the garden, whilst Marcus was leisurely putting on his coat.

"I am afraid I shall take cold if I go out in my shirt-sleeves," said Marcus, "it's a very bad plan to——"

"Stop thief!" shouted Mr. Oliver, plunging

into the garden, coatless himself, and then a little scream from the drawing-room announced that the ladies had caught the alarm.

It was all the work of a moment; Mr. Slitherwick had secured the offender, who, making no effort to run away, had leisurely waited for his pursuer to come up with him. Captor and captive returned to the billiard-room, followed by Mr. Oliver; three or four scared servants appeared upon the scene, and Fanny and her mother, both very pale, entered from the drawing-room and added to the number.

"Who are you? What do you want in my garden? Send for a policeman, somebody," cried Mr. Oliver, putting on his coat. "Will somebody go for a policeman, or not?"

"One moment, Mr. Oliver," said Mr. Slitherwick, "I think, if you'll allow me to suggest, it may be as well to hear what the boy has to say?"

"What the thief has to say, you mean," said the manufacturer.

The boy stood with his hands in his pockets, glancing furtively from Mr. Oliver to Mr.

Slitherwick, and from Mr. Slitherwick to Mr.
Oliver, as each spoke in turn, and it was a very
hang-dog glance that was directed from under
his pent-house brows, and the tangled matted
hair which was pulled over his low forehead.

"I ain't done no harm to yer, yer needn't
fetch the coppers to me—the genelman told
me to wait, didn't he?" said Larry, sullenly, as
he rubbed one bare, dirty foot over the other.

"What gentleman?" asked Mr. Oliver.

"I don't know what genelman," said Larry,
passing the back of his hand over his broken
nose and sniffing violently; "I ain't done
nuffink but bring a messidge to a lady. I was
to wait for a hanswer, and a bloomin' nice
time she's been about it too."

"A message to a lady—what lady?"

"I don't know what lady—he did," answered
Larry. "He tooked the letter and told me to
wait in the garding, and gord's truth I've been
a-waiting, I have!"

"Bless my soul and body, it's very remarkable!" said Mr. Oliver. "What kind of a gentleman was he?"

"I don't see him here," replied Larry, with a quick and comprehensive look round. "Ain't a bit like any of you blokes."

"I suppose it's Tom," suggested Marcus.

"How did you get here?" asked Mr. Oliver.

"He let me in at the stable door when I rang," said Larry, making his first departure from the strict truth, and it was to his mind a very necessary precaution under the circumstances.

"What did he want at the stable door, I wonder?" said Mr. Oliver, scratching his head vigorously.

"I daresay he went round to see Cabbage," Marcus replied, after a moment's thought.

"To see a cabbage! Good gracious, are you mad too?" exclaimed Mr. Oliver. "What cabbage?"

"That's the name of his dog," said Marcus.

"Oh, ah! Then why didn't you say so? It's very extraordinary and mysterious," said Mr. Oliver; "it's all——"

"There's the cove—there's the cove; that's *him!*" cried Larry, with a sudden yelp of ex-

citement that made everybody jump, and. then
Tom Dagnell was seen standing in the doorway,
very white and stern.

"What does all this mean?" inquired Tom.

"We—we caught this boy in the garden, Mr.
Dagnell," said Mr. Oliver; "he says you let
him in, took a message from him, and told him
to wait for an answer."

"Quite right," said Tom, quietly; "I was
feeding Cab when the lad rang at the bell. I
let him in, and carried his message to Miss Hilderbrandt. There was a poor woman—one of
Miss Hilderbrandt's pensioners—taken seriously
ill, and Miss Hilderbrandt thought she should
like to see her, and went off in haste. I accompanied her, and we both forgot the
boy.

"Has Miss Hilderbrandt returned?" asked
Fanny Oliver.

"Yes—she is in the drawing-room."

"Oh! I am so glad," cried Fanny; "I will go
to her directly. Pa dear, give the boy a shilling or two for me," and away bustled Fanny

in search of her new friend. "He's had a terrible fright, poor lad!"

"I'll see to the boy, Miss Oliver," said Tom; then he beckoned to Larry, who slouched across the room with the same furtive looks, and followed him into the hall, where Tom was now standing with the door open.

"I should have told you not to wait," said Tom to the boy; "here's half-a-crown for forgetting you."

"Thankee, guv'nor," said the boy, with a hungry snatch at the coin.

"I may want you again. Where do you live?"

"In the Inkleys."

"What number?"

"Oh! anybody can tell you where to find Larry," said the boy. He spat on his half-crown, tossed it in the air, caught it, thrust it into his pocket, and darted out of the house along the carriage drive, and through the open gates into the Hagley Road, down which he ran at full speed towards the town—a lad anxious to make up for lost time.

Tom closed the door after him, and then with the same stern face walked slowly and thoughtfully towards the drawing-room.

CHAPTER XVIII.

RECONCILIATION.

THE harmony of the evening had been too seriously disturbed for the Oliver family and their guests to settle down before the hour for rest. Mr. Oliver had been unduly excited, and had had visions of housebreakers planning an attack upon his premises, and it had all resolved itself into a ragged boy waiting for a message in the back garden, an odd proceeding in itself, but not worth the noise which had been made about it. Fanny Oliver endeavoured to treat the whole affair as a jest now, but found no one prepared to second her; Marcus returned to his old place, and to his old dozing attitude; Miss Oliver was curious about the sick woman whom Miss Hilderbrandt had visited, and was scarcely satisfied by hearing that the invalid was better; Tom sat with the same heavy frown on his face, although ostensibly interested in a volume of John Leech's sketches, which he had taken from the drawing-room table, and was studying with a scowl.

"I think it is time we made a move, Mrs. O.," said Mr. Oliver, with a yawn, "unless anybody cares for whist."

Nobody caring for whist, Mr. and Mrs. Oliver were the first to prepare for departure, the head of the house giving his final instructions to his daughter.

"See the servants lock the house up all right, Fanny; that blackguard boy has made me nervous," he said, with a short laugh, "and there's a sight of plate about."

"It's all counted, papa, and shall be locked up before I go to bed."

"There's a good child. She'll make a wonderful housekeeper, Marco, ha! ha!" he said, with his old cheerful laugh returning. "Good night, Marcus; good night, Master Tom; good night, Miss Hilderbrandt."

He shook hands formally with each one whom he addressed, kissed his daughter affectionately as a wind up, and withdrew, followed by Mrs. Oliver, who went through the same ceremonious programme.

Marcus Dagnell rose a few minutes afterwards, and at a telegraphic signal from Fanny, which rendered him wide awake at once.

"Are you ready, Tom?" he inquired.

"Presently," said Tom, without looking up from his book, "I am busy just now."

"Are you, really?" said Marcus. "I'll bid you good night, then."

Marcus bowed politely over the hand of Miss Hilderbrandt and went out, and Fanny, after muttering something about the servants, and returning in a minute, followed him from the drawing-room.

"Well, now, really, Fanny, this is very kind of you," said Marcus, a fit of affection seizing him on the mat outside, as he attempted to take hold of Fanny's hand.

"Don't be silly, Marcus, at this time of night," said Fanny, with a slap to his face which he thought was a trifle too spiteful; "do you think I have been running out of the room after you, you big stupid?"

"What is it, then?"

"Don't you see they've had a little tiff about something," explained Fanny, "a few words about your precious cousin Ursula, I know; and I want to give them a chance of making it up again."

"Well, but look here——"

"There, good night, you goose," cried Fanny, pushing him towards the staircase, "you don't understand these things so well as I do. Let me be now, I'm going to count the silver."

"One chaste salute, Fanny, before I retire," said the amorous Marcus, gently detaining her.

"No, no, no, no!" said Fanny, very rapidly.

"Just to make up for this dreadful evening."

"What dreadful evening?"

"It's always dreadful when that Slither-wick——"

"I'll not hear another word against papa's friend," cried Fanny. "It is not kind of you, at all."

Fanny flounced herself away from him at this, and Marcus, after a sad shake of his head, went slowly to his room.

Meanwhile, Tom Dagnell and Violet Hilderbrandt were left together in the drawing-room to make their peace with each other. It had been kindly planned by the astute Miss Oliver, who had seen further into their feelings than had the rest of the community. Yes, there was something wrong—there had arisen a difference between them—the shadow no larger than one's hand was spreading balefully above them both.

It was the lady who made the first advances to reconciliation; who rose immediately as the door closed behind Fanny, and came and stood humbly before our hero.

"You have lost faith in me very quickly, Mr. Dagnell," she said, in a low tone of reproach.

"I am surprised—I am perplexed," Tom

confessed, as he closed his book and looked steadily at her in return.

"Will you not wait for my explanation, and till I have seen your cousin Ursula?" she asked —"will you not keep your word with me?"

"Certainly, Miss Hilderbrandt," was Tom's reply. "I do not seek—I do not ask for your confidence."

"But you cannot trust in me—you, the one friend who came to my rescue!"

The voice broke a little, and the hands were wrung together as if in pain.

Tom was moved.

"I can only say I do not understand what is going on, and that you are a riddle to me which I shall never solve," said Tom.

"Ah, yes, you will," Violet replied, sadly, "and that very soon."

"If I have lost faith, Miss Hilderbrandt, it is only in your discretion," said Tom; "you act rashly and without consulting me—me, whom you sent for because of the danger which threatened you."

"Yes."

"And yet that danger you went forth this evening to seek voluntarily."

"No," was Violet's answer, "I did not."

"I have been trying to screen you. For the first time in my life, I have deliberately lied," said Tom, bitterly; "and if I had any pride in me at all, it was in being above a lie."

"I am sorry—I am very sorry—that you should have defended the boy, or attempted to explain his presence here," said Violet. "I did not ask you to do that, Mr. Dagnell, but—forgive me!"

She extended her right hand to him, and he held it in his own for a moment. When she had withdrawn it, she passed it quickly across her eyes, which were wet with sudden tears.

"I wish I had gone away this morning," she murmured, sitting in the vacant chair facing him; "why did I stop, I wonder?"

"I persuaded you," replied Tom; "possibly I was wrong. Was it necessary to meet this stranger?"

"It was necessary," replied Violet. "I was found out—my father would have come next."

"And you fear him?"

"Yes, at times. Not always." .

"And you were terribly afraid of meeting him yesterday—he was your one fear—your——"

"No, no, Mr. Dagnell," she said, interrupting him. "You mistake me, as you mistake the motive of my life. He menaces me with no danger. I may be afraid of him in my heart, but I am not anxious to hide from him."

Tom Dagnell drew a deep breath of astonishment.

"Then it is not he——" he began.

"He is more afraid of me than I am of him," said Violet Hilderbrandt; "he warns me of my danger, not brings danger to me—that I am aware," she added, after a moment's pause.

"I am in the clouds," Tom confessed. "I will not attempt to pierce them."

"You will trust me still," she added, very anxiously, "for one day longer—till your cousin asks me to come to her, or tells me not to come? Ah, Mr. Dagnell, don't turn against me! Keep your faith in me for a little while. You are the only friend in England I have."

The entreaty was too earnest for Tom to hold out against; the face of Violet was possibly too beautiful for Tom to gaze at long without feeling all his sense of mistrust vanishing away like snowflakes in the sun. The truth was surely shining from those large dark eyes, which looked at him unflinchingly, and claimed his faith in her as her lawful right.

"Miss Hilderbrandt, I do not doubt you," he said, "and I will wait your own time for explanation."

"Thank you," she answered. Their hands met again in sign of this new pledge of confidence between them, and there was a brighter smile upon her face than he had witnessed hitherto. Miss Oliver came in, and found them shaking hands together, and looking kindly at each other.

"Oh! I beg pardon," she said, dryly; "but it *is* getting late, you know."

There was no response; indeed it was exceedingly difficult to respond to Miss Oliver's last remark.

When adieux for the night had been exchanged, and Violet Hilderbrandt and Fanny were in the corridor, and close to the doors of their respective rooms, Fanny made an impulsive little dash at Violet, and embraced her warmly.

"I am so glad you have made it up with him," said Fanny. "Oh, you don't know how glad I am!"

Violet was surprised, but she murmured,

"We had not quarrelled, Miss Oliver."

"Ah! there was something, I'm sure," said Fanny, "and, as you have made it up again, I don't much mind what it was. Good night, dear."

"Good night, dear," Violet echoed back.

"Oh!—and I say," remarked Fanny, stealing to her side again on tiptoe, "don't you think anything about that cousin of his. It's all a mistake, I am sure. I have seen her, and it isn't at all likely. It is not, indeed!"

Fanny darted into her room immediately

after this suggestive remark, and left Violet Hilderbrandt to reflect upon the advice which had been proffered her.

CHAPTER XIX.

THE NIGHT ALARM.

OUR hero was glad to be alone to think over the events of the day, and to wonder whither they were leading him. The man who hated mystery was battling as vainly to escape it, as a traveller might from a treacherous bog-land upon which he had incautiously ventured.

Tom sat back in the easy-chair at the foot of his bed, lighted a cigar, and composed himself to review the case as best he might, and with that limited idea of the prospect which he appeared to possess. He did not attempt to solve further the problem of Violet Hilderbrandt's position—he had promised her the faith to wait —but he looked back upon all that had hap-

pened, and wondered whether it were for good
or evil, so far as her young life was concerned.
Were the clouds clearing, or deepening? Was
hope approaching more closely, or fading away
into the background of the night?

He could think of nothing else save Violet
Hilderbrandt. What a hold she had taken of
his thoughts!—he might have known her for
years, considering how deeply interested he
was in everything she did and said. Could he
even account for the distress which he had ex-
perienced in witnessing her sorrow at his distrust, which had never lain at the bottom of his
heart, for all his doubtful words? Ah! no more
than he could account for the faith which he
had promised should abide with him, and for
which she had shown her gratitude that night.
How glad he should be when the story was
clear, and he could sympathize with the troubles
of her past, and tell what was best for her in
the future! He was not a wise man, but he
thought he could predict what was best, and
she would believe him and follow his counsel—
and Ursula's! Ah! Ursula. A wise woman

with a tender heart disguised by a semblance of asceticism—if she would " take to " Violet and love her—if she would only be her true, deep feeling self to a young girl unutterably alone!

He smoked his cigar out, lighted another, and went on with his reverie. It was pleasant to sit there and think of Violet Hilderbrandt. Amongst the little accomplishments of which he had been prone to boast was that of his power to endure fatigue, being young and strong, and in full health, and it had not struck him that last night had been long and toilsome, that he had risen early, and there had indeed been little rest for him since he had said good-bye to Ursula at Broadlands. He had no consciousness of fatigue, but he dropped off suddenly to sleep in the capacious chair at the bed's foot, and dreamed that Ursula and Violet were bosom friends, and were wandering about the fair home park lands, with arms twined round each other's waists, true sisters in affection. Quite a happy dream, with all the troubles set away in the background for good, and all the ministers of evil, Hilderbrandt and Co., and Larry, he could see Larry in their midst, cowering in the distance, and hindered from advancing one step forward into the brightness of the present by Cabbage—faithful Cabbage, who, with his forelegs planted wide apart, opened his big, black mouth, and bayed at them.

He bayed so long and furiously that Tom Dagnell woke up with the noise, and found that it was part of actual life beyond the dreamland into which he had drifted.

Cabbage, in real earnest, was barking in the rear of the premises, his loud deep notes reverberating painfully at that late hour. Tom sat up to listen; he sprang to his feet to make sure; a suspicion of danger was upon him; he had heard so much of danger lately, and had travelled so far from the ordinary routine of his life to meet it, that he was preternaturally on the alert. He had made one step towards the window, when the door, which he had not locked for the night, opened suddenly, and a lank, slippered figure in extraordinary attire came in.

"Marcus!" exclaimed Tom, "what's the

matter?   Why are you dressed in this mounte-
bank fashion?"

" I'm not dressed at all.   I put the first thing
on, I could find in the dark.   I've had a sort of
fright," said Marcus, " being taken off my
guard, and without a light.   I'm very glad
you're up, Tom."

Tom Dagnell looked at Marcus, and burst
into a hearty laugh.   There might be more
mystery, even a tragedy to come, but the burlesque of the present situation it was impossible
to resist.   Marcus had slipped out of bed in a
most voluminous night-shirt, and put on a pair
of slippers, a high-crowned hat, and the dress-
coat he had worn at dinner, and in this extem-
pore guise he had shuffled from his own room,
along the corridor, and to Tom's apartment.

" I don't know what you can see to laugh
at," said Marcus, gravely surveying his brother,
" and it is not quite the time of night to make
that confounded row.   Haven't you heard the
dog?"

" Yes, he awoke me."

" Why, you have not been to bed!" said
Marcus, with surprise.

"No, I dozed off in the chair."

"I suppose you are not ridiculous enough to walk in your sleep; it wasn't you?" said Marcus, still a little doubtfully.

"It wasn't I—what?" asked Tom, quickly.

"Somebody has been in my room," replied Marcus. "I heard a kind of a chink on the toilet-table, and that woke me up. I asked who was there, but nobody answered me. It couldn't be——"

Tom seized his match-box, and hurried into the corridor without waiting for further details, and Marcus followed him to the apartment which he had recently quitted.

Tom ignited a match, and lighted one of the gas-burners by the side of Marcus's toilet-glass. There was no one in the room, but there were evident signs of a visitor having intruded therein. Marcus's clothes, all of which, after his usual custom, had been carefully folded before retiring to rest, were pitched about the carpet and into the fireplace, a pair of black trousers, with the whole length of the white linings of the pockets exposed to view, being particularly suggestive of the spoiler.

"Thieves!" ejaculated Marcus, "and they've cleared me out, too! There's my watch gone off the table—it was a magnificent lever, Tom, wasn't it?—and my ring—and——" here he took his shirt from the fender, and looked down ruefully at the crumpled front, "and my diamond studs, by gad! Isn't it positively awful?"

"Yes. Dress yourself decently, and join me downstairs. I am afraid this is not the end of it."

"What—what do you think?"

"That poor old Oliver has been robbed, and yours is a mere supplement to it all," answered Tom, sternly.

"It's very fine of you to call it a mere supplement. I think——"

But Tom had not waited to hear all that was in the thoughts of Marcus Dagnell—he had passed out of the room and along the corridor to the broad landing-place, leaving his brother to join him as speedily as he might consider necessary under the circumstances. The gas was burning dimly in the corridor, but the hall was a deep well of blackness, into which he peered over the balusters. On the stairs were many signs of disorder; papers and odd books were scattered down them, and at his feet was a silver fork, which had been dropped in haste by hands not generally disposed to be careless when silver was in question.

"Have you got them—have you found anything more?" asked Marcus, as he joined his brother, fully equipped.

"There has been a great robbery," said Tom; "all the plate has been stolen, I'm afraid. Here's a fork dropped by one of the housebreakers."

"Perhaps they've dropped my studs," said Marcus, glancing wildly round, but in vain.

"Wake Mr. Oliver and the servants, whilst I go downstairs and look about me," said Tom. "The thieves have been alarmed,

and may yet be secured. Tell somebody to
run outside and find the police, too—look
sharp!"

Tom hurried downstairs full of excitement,
and of eagerness to secure the robbers, if it were
possible; with the matches in his case he lighted
the gas here and there as he proceeded, and
with every step he came upon fresh proof of
wreckage, but no trace of the wreckers. The
drawing-room was open—it was by that means
an entrance had been effected—and Tom saw
that the window was wide open also, with the
night and the stars for a background. He passed into the garden, echoing still with Cabbage's
loud barking from the stableyard, but all was
desolate and black, although there were many
signs of crushed plants and trampled flower-
beds. When he returned to the house there
was a crowd of men and women with white
faces and glaring eyes to receive him—
the host and hostess, and their servants,
together with Marcus, Fanny, and Violet
Hilderbrandt. Some one had set an alarm-bell
·ringing also from a little turret over the princi-

pal stable, and it sounded like a death-knell at that hour. There was trouble in the house of Oliver.

CHAPTER XX.

MR. OLIVER'S LOSSES.

IT was a strange, excited group of men and women that stood in the drawing-room of Elmslie House, looking from one to another for support and consolation. The surprise was too great, the shock too close at hand, for each to assume quickly his or her natural character. There was a blank stupefaction reigning supreme over most of the community. Presently some one lighted the burners in the great gas chandelier, and gave quite a festive air to the scene, and Tom said,

"They came in through these windows, it is evident. Have you searched the house? Do you know what is lost?"

"Do I know what isn't lost, you mean," rejoined Mr. Oliver, as he sat down on the couch and mopped his forehead with his silk handkerchief; "or what hasn't gone?"

"Oh! dear," said Mrs. Oliver, taking a place very close to her husband's side, as befitted a helpmate in affliction; "you mustn't worry about this, Jonathan. It's all sent for our good: that is, it's all gone away for our good, depend upon it."

"Yes, it's all gone away—in cart-loads," assented Mr. Oliver, with a groan.

"Every scrap of plate, too," said Fanny.

"And the chest it was in, cut up like so much cheese," added Mr. Oliver.

"And my watch, and a set of diamond studs," Marcus ventured to remark; "as if they could not have left them alone."

"And—Lord save us!—look there, my Turner!" ejaculated Mr. Oliver. "Oh! my poor Turner."

Yes; they were certainly thieves of rare discrimination who had paid a visit to Mr. Oliver's Edgbaston mansion; there was a taste for the fine arts in their midst, a keen appreciation of the True, the Beautiful, and the Sublime—Mr. Oliver's Turner picture, the gem of his collection, the canvas representative of some three thousand pounds odd at the last sale, and worth another thousand, knowing people thought, had been carefully cut from its frame, rolled up, and carried off with the rest of the property.

"By gad!" exclaimed Marcus, looking at the empty gilt frame hanging from the wall, "that's following the fashion in burglary, at any rate."

"This is not the time for irony, Mr. Dagnell," said Mr. Oliver, "and although I'm not a ruined man, I don't consider it friendly to make remarks like that on the present occasion."

"I was only thinking——" began Marcus.

"Please don't think of anything but how to capture the ruffian. Is *all* the plate gone, Fanny?" inquired Mr. Oliver. "Did I hear you say every scrap?"

"Yes, papa. Oh! I'm so dreadfully frightened."

"They've collared my testimonial, then?" said Mr. Oliver, with a sigh. "Centre piece— it was on the supper-table last night. It was worth four hundred pounds, that was."

"I wonder what they'll do with it?" said Marcus. "They can't make use of it very often!"

"They'll melt it down, sir. We have every convenience for melting metals in Birmingham, I can assure you," replied Mr. Oliver, severely. "Has anyone gone for the police?"

Yes, three or four servants had sallied forth in different directions in search of the constabulary of the borough. Meanwhile, there was nothing to be done but wander in a helpless fashion about the house and garden, in search of further loss, or of fresh proof of detection. Tom walked across to Violet Hilderbrandt, after a few words of condolence with Mr. Oliver, and sat down by her side. She was as pale as the rest, but apparently very calm.

"This robbery has not alarmed you, I am glad to see," he said.

"No, I am not alarmed," was the reply slowly vouchsafed to him.

"I am glad of that," replied Tom ; "did the dog wake you?"

"I was not asleep," said Violet. "I had not thought of sleep."

"You might have heard the noises in the house."

"I went once to my door to listen," she answered.

"Half an hour earlier, a quarter of an hour, and we should have captured the thieves!" exclaimed Tom.

"God forbid!" she murmured.

"Miss Hilderbrandt!" exclaimed Tom.

"Hush! don't speak so loud—don't look at me like that," she said, in a suppressed voice. "You cannot suspect me of any connivance in this villainy?"

"Oh! Miss Hilderbrandt, is that possible?"

"They may do so presently," she whispered, with a glance at the others arguing and explaining and comparing notes. "What is to hinder them? Ah, Mr. Dagnell, it was not prudent to come to this unlucky house."

"Where was the mistake?" he asked.

"It was dangerous—it was an unwise step," she replied. "I am helpless here—without a friend—save you. I left the house clandestinely this evening, and met a strange man in the Hagley Road. I returned to find a lad had been captured in my absence, and that you were accounting for his appearance here. That boy is known to the police as one of a desperate gang of thieves, and will be captured possibly. What will he say?"

"What can he say?"

"I do not know. I am afraid, but it is not for myself now."

"For your father?"

"No—for you."

"For me!" exclaimed Tom Dagnell.

"You spoke to the boy in the garden," Violet continued, in a low whisper. "They will say you let him in; it will be disproved that he brought a message from a sick dependent—you were the first moving in the house again. God forgive me, I have dragged you, my one friend, into the eternal misery of my life!"

"Miss Hilderbrandt, for your own sake be silent. Do not fear for me—think of yourself," replied Tom. "If I have approached to-night more closely to the secret of that life, I may be more of service."

"Yes, it is easy to guess all now, and yet so easy to misjudge me—which you will not," she added, "for of this dark night's work I did not dream."

"Heaven forbid I should think you did!" said Tom, earnestly.

"You trust me still?"

"Implicitly. Have I not given you my word?"

"It was before this."

"I shall never doubt you again," he whispered.

"I am deeply grateful," she answered, in the same tone and breath. "The time may come to repay it in some way or fashion hidden from me now. I hope it will."

It was a strange dialogue, hastily whispered in the big drawing-room, where there had been much revelry four and twenty hours ago;

but there was no one to hear them, or to
wonder at their subject of discourse. The
robbery was the one absorbing theme, and the
centre of attraction was the robbed man sitting
with a hand on each knee and his arms akimbo,
after a habit that he had ; Mrs. Oliver was by
his side, disposed towards hysterics, but forti-
fied with a glass of cold brandy and water which
some good Samaritan had placed within her
reach ; the servants were still debating, or
walking from drawing-room to garden and
back again, as though they were invited guests
to an *al fresco* entertainment ; Tom's mastiff,
excited again by various noises, had burst
forth into renewed protests against the dis-
turbers of his rest ; Fanny Oliver was in a
corner, receiving consolation from Marcus, who
had turned the collar of his coat about his ears
as a protection against the night air, which
came in gustily through the windows that Mr.
Oliver would not have closed until the police
had arrived and seen them open. They came
at last, two men in uniform and an inspector in
private clothes, the latter a busy man who took

sundry notes, and asked a variety of questions of Marcus, Tom, and the servants.

"You were the first to find any trace of the burglars?" he inquired of our hero.

Tom answered in the affirmative, and at the officer's request entered into the details of his discovery.

"You were sitting up, then?" was the next question.

"Yes."

The note-book was in requisition again.

"You reached Birmingham by the 12.15 train last night, and took a cab to Acock's Green, I think, Mr. Dagnell?"

Tom was surprised, but he nodded his head in assent.

"Thank you; that will do," said the inspector.

The note-book was dropped into a side pocket, and its owner whispered a few words to Mr. Oliver, who rose and said, "Certainly, certainly," and walked with him into the library, where Tom had written his letter to Ursula that morning.

" You'll excuse. me, sir, I am sure," said the inspector, politely; " no offence meant is no offence given, and we are compelled to ask a goodish many questions in a big job of this kind."

" It's a big job, and a bad job too," replied Mr. Oliver; " what do you want to ask ?"

" This Mr. Dagnell; you have known him a long time, I suppose ?"

" Which Mr. Dagnell ?"

" The one who sat up late to-night."

" Known him long!   Well, I have known his family a long time."

" Yes, but the gentleman himself ?"

" I remember him as a boy," was the reply; "but he came here last night for the first time. Why, you can't think——"

" No, I don't think anything; I don't say anything," said the officer, very quickly; " it is not at all likely I should, but we are compelled to ask all kinds of questions.   Where does he live, as a rule ?"

" He's the son of Sir John Dagnell, Broad-lands, Sussex—his elder brother is going to marry my daughter," said Mr. Oliver, with a sudden burst of information, "you are labouring under a delusion, and a very great one, if you think for a moment——"

"I don't think," said the inspector, producing his note-book again, and entering Tom's address very carefully. "I keep telling you, sir, it's not my business to think, only to ask questions. This Mr. Dagnell whose Christian name you say is Richard——"

"I never said anything of the kind," interrupted Mr. Oliver, "his name is Thomas Dagnell."

"Thomas, thank you," said the officer, booking it at once, "I certainly thought you mentioned the name of Richard. Well, the gentleman will be a most important witness, if we are fortunate enough to catch the thieves. By the way," he added, as a second thought appeared to suggest itself, "you had a little fright earlier in the evening, the servants tell me?"

"Yes, there was a boy found on the premises," said Mr. Oliver.

"How did he account for being there?"

" He rang at the side-bell. Mr. Dagnell was in the stable-yard feeding his dog, so he let him in," said Mr. Oliver.

" What did the boy want?" was the next question.

"I don't know. He brought a message to a lady who is staying with us," was the reply.

" And then he went away again."

" No; that's what he did not do," and Mr. Oliver entered into an explanation of the boy's capture at a later hour.

" Would you know the boy again?"

" Anywhere."

" Any distinguishing mark at all?"

" The bridge of his nose is broken, I fancy."

"Larry Simes," muttered the inspector to himself. He asked a few more questions, and then put away his note-book for good.

"You'll offer a reward, Mr. Oliver, I suppose?" he said.

" I'll offer a thousand pounds reward, two thousand, anything to catch the thieves," cried the manufacturer.

"A hundred, or a couple of hundred, will be quite sufficient to begin with, if you will allow me to make a suggestion, Mr. Oliver."

"Very well, say two hundred," replied the other.

"Of course, everything I have said is in perfect confidence between us, Mr. Oliver," added the policeman. "You won't repeat to anybody the questions I have put to you. I wouldn't, sir, if I was you—I wouldn't, indeed."

"You can trust me to keep my own counsel," he answered.

The inspector was withdrawing, when the manufacturer called him back.

"Make every inquiry you can, but don't bill the walls with—with that reward we spoke of, just yet," Mr. Oliver said, stammering somewhat as he spoke. "You can come and talk to me again about this—and as soon as you have anything to tell me—but don't bill the walls. I don't want everybody in Birmingham to know I have been robbed, and I—I haven't made up my mind quite as to the amount I shall offer for the conviction of the blackguards. You won't lose anything by this, Mr.——what's your name?"

" Critchett, sir."

" You understand," he said; " I'd rather talk this over again, when I'm less bothered, d'ye see?"

" Yes, sir, I think I comprehend."

Mr. Critchett took his departure; the policemen, overborne with details, followed in his wake; the house was locked up once more; the gas was turned off in the various rooms; the servants walked reluctantly away; the guests withdrew with more condolences, and Mr. Oliver still sat in his library, in his old attitude, and with his big, broad face full of deep concern.

It was his faithful better half who found him there at last.

" Hadn't you better come upstairs and rest a bit till morning, Jonathan?" she asked.

" I think I had," he said, but he did not move for all that.

" It's a great loss," continued the consoler, "but it won't come heavy-like upon us. We can afford it, Jonathan, if anybody can. It might have been some poor fellow living up to the last penny of his income, or who had sunk his capital in forks and spoons, mightn't it?"

"I don't care about the plate," Mr. Oliver said. in a deep bass voice; "I'd rather it had been twenty times as much if——"

He paused, and his wife said:

"If the picture hadn't gone. Ah! well, it might have been a prettier picture, goodness knows, and much good may it do those who've got it. I never liked that picture."

"Mrs. Oliver," said her lord and husband, gravely, "you are talking about what you don't understand."

"Yes, I know I am; but you are fretting, Jonathan, and I don't like to see it."

"I'm not fretting about a picture or the trumpery silver, ma'am," he replied, "but at the wickedness of the world, and there's an awful lot of it about—an awful lot, I can tell you, Polly."

And, with this moral reflection and stern truth, Mr. Oliver allowed himself to be led to his room.

CHAPTER XXI.

TWO FATHERS.

IF Mr. Oliver had calculated upon keeping the fact of the robbery of his premises a secret between him and the police, he had certainly reckoned without his host. The ill news flew apace after the custom of its kind; the newspapers pounced upon the incident; people were talking of it in the morning at the corners of the streets, in all the factories, and at all the breakfast-tables of busy Birmingham, and when Mr. Oliver drove to the manufactory in his carriage, he felt that he was a greater object of interest than ordinary, and regarded, not only as the rich man who had risen from the ranks, and whom honest folk regarded none the less for that, but with some sympathy and human interest as a man who had been cruelly despoiled. He was not quite himself that day at the great establishment, where he was always at his best, and where the dish-cover business went on by wholesale—where a thousand hands were hard at work in his especial service, and the rattle, rattle of innumerable machines kept on unceasingly, twisting, grinding, shaping, and polishing metal into a marketable commodity. He had something on his mind, and those who were ungenerous enough to think he was brooding on his loss at Edgbaston were very much mistaken, and should have known the master better. It was, as he had owned in general terms to his wife, the wickedness of the world which had appalled and depressed him—although he had not allowed it to disturb him in business hours before, and only for a short while in church, between eleven and one on Sunday mornings, when the weather was tolerably fine.

Certainly the world's wickedness had come home to him, but Mr. Oliver was scarcely the man to fret about that even, most people would have considered. Still he plodded through his workshops with only half a business eye to the labour in his service—the shrewd, all round glance which nothing escaped, was not perceptible that morning, nor the usual friendly nod and cheerful word to his subordinates, nor the interest in their work, which he was always ready to assume. He had no questions to ask; he did not stop to give one order, or to point out one mistake; he went back to his counting-house and his books, and let the dish-covers increase and multiply without his fostering care—for the first time in his life he allowed the foremen to have it all their own way, and the machinery to grind on without comment on his part. It was eleven o'clock in the morning when a card was brought to him from the outer office.

"If it's anyone who wants to go over the works, he can go," said Mr. Oliver, listlessly. "Don't worry me to-day, Robins."

"He says his business is with you particularly," replied the messenger.

"Oh, then it's——" Mr. Oliver looked at the

card and said, "Oh, no—it isn't. Is he a gentleman in appearance, Robins?"

"Yes, sir, quite the gentleman," was the reply. "He's come in a carriage and pair, with livery servants, and all that."

"Show him up. '*Mr. Hilderbrandt,*'" said Mr. Oliver, reading the card again, and on this occasion aloud. "Why didn't he go to Elmslie House, I wonder?"

He put his pen behind his ear and waited patiently for his visitor, who was shortly afterwards ushered in—a being resplendent in the first style of fashion, and carrying in a lavender-gloved hand the glossiest of silk hats.

"I am sorry to trouble you, Mr. Oliver—I am extremely sorry to intrude upon you in hours of business, and on a domestic matter that is purely personal to myself," he said, after a profuse bow, and in a slightly foreign accent, "but necessity—urgency—must plead my excuse."

"Take a seat," said Mr. Oliver. "You are related to Miss Hilderbrandt, I presume?"

"I am her father, sir. I have the honour, I may add—for she is a genius—to be the parent of that gifted girl," replied Mr. Hilderbrandt, as he sat down at the manufacturer's request.

"I am glad of that," said Mr. Oliver. "I was afraid you were after a subscription, and I am not in a charitable mood this morning."

"Indeed," was Mr. Hilderbrandt's answer, "you very much surprise me. The fame of Mr. Oliver as a liberal benefactor, a supporter of institutions, not entirely local, even, is far from unknown to me."

"I can put my money down when there's a good cause for it, as well as any man in Birmingham," said Mr. Oliver. "You have heard as much, I don't doubt."

"I have," replied Mr. Hilderbrandt. "But I have not come to levy blackmail on your benevolence, or to take up any great measure of your time, which is money to you also."

"Exactly, sir. Thank you," said Mr. Oliver. "We are always busy here. As the father of Miss Hilderbrandt, I should have been pleased to see you at Elmslie House, where your daughter is now staying."

"A thousand thanks, Mr. Oliver. Allow me to

press your hand for one instant in token of my gratitude," he said, rising and shaking hands with the manufacturer forthwith, and then resuming his seat. "Had it been in my power, I should have been extremely happy to pay a visit to your home. But my child—my only child—and I are not friends, sir."

There were tears in the black eyes of Mr. Hilderbrandt, one of them coursed slowly down the left side of his nose as he spoke, and Mr. Oliver saw it, and was affected immediately.

"God bless my soul—you don't say so?" he exclaimed, interested at once in his visitor and the object of his visit. "I am extremely sorry to hear it; so nice a young lady, too! Go on, sir; what can I do? I am the father of an only child myself, and shall be glad to hear in what way I can act as a medium between you and your daughter. Dear me—dear me—think of that now!"

"You are more than kind to me, you are an English gentleman, indeed," said Mr. Hilderbrandt, dashing another tear from his eye.

"I am only an English manufacturer, sir—

only Dish-cover Oliver, as they call me in Warwickshire," he said, with a modesty which
might have been a trifle affected; "pray proceed."

"My daughter left home, without her parents'
consent, two or three months ago, partly im-
pelled by a craze for popularity, and in order to
seek that applause for her abilities which the
world can bestow more effectively than friends at
home; and partly, I fear, prompted to her rash
act by one who has too sure a hold upon her
affections."

"You—you don't mean——"

"Oh! sir, I have come here without disguise.
I am a very plain man, and speak plainly," said
Mr. Hilderbrandt. "I allude to Mr. Thomas
Dagnell, a desperate young fellow, with prin-
ciples perverted by bad company, and a loose
and profligate life upon the Continent—a ne'er-
do-weel who was turned away from home five
years ago for robbing his own father—a villain
whose specious ways have got that command
over my child which it is beyond my power to
foil without the aid of good and true men like

yourself, who can realize the dreadful position in which I am unfortunately placed.”

“ You amaze me,” said Mr. Oliver, very short of breath now, “you utterly amaze me, sir. So bad as that, is he?”

“ He has been the companion of thieves and reprobates abroad—he has been wholly desperate.”

“ Good gracious!”

“ And he seeks my daughter only for her riches,” continued the fluent Mr. Hilderbrandt. “ I am wealthy, and she will become naturally my heiress. She is very weak, and this *miserable* exerts a fascination over her which influences every step in her life. Now, sir,” with both hands outspread, and the one which held the hat shaking very much, “ what am I to do?”

“ I don’t quite see. I——”

“ I have come over from Paris, where I am principal of one of the largest firms in the world, perhaps—Hilderbrandt and Jardine, general merchants—at great inconvenience and loss, to see my child once more, and make one last appeal to her to return with me to Paris, and her mother."

"She is at Elmslie House—I think I have told you before? But upon my soul," Mr. Oliver blurted forth, "I hardly know what I have told you, and what I haven't, you run on at such a rate!"

"Yes, sir, you have told me she is at Elmslie House," said Mr. Hilderbrandt, disconsolately, "but that I knew already. It is the opportunity of seeing her in private—when that wretched man is not present—that I require, that I ask of you as the greatest favour one gentleman can confer upon another."

"That is easily managed," said Mr. Oliver.

"She will listen to a father's voice, a father's entreaty, I am sure, if I can only speak with her alone. I hope and pray she will not be deaf to reason, but be prepared to accompany me at once. For oh!" he cried, in a burst of enthusiasm, "she is a gentle, truthful, amiable girl, she loved us all so very much, we were all so proud of her and her accomplishments; she was the one bright light of home!"

"Yes, yes, I perfectly understand. I see," said Mr. Oliver, wiping his eyes, and blowing his nose violently. "You can come round this evening, and ask for me privately. I'll contrive that you shall meet your daughter, sir. It is my duty."

Mr. Hilderbrandt rose, and held out his hand to Mr. Oliver again.

"It is your duty, but I know not how to thank you," he said, in a voice very much broken with emotion, "I cannot tell how to thank you yet."

"Don't mention it," said Mr. Oliver.

"Ask to see you privately, I think you said— and at Elmslie House, Hagley Road? A million thanks, sir," he murmured forth, "but this Thomas Dagnell will be on the alert. His cunning is that of the evil one itself."

"Leave it to me," said Mr. Oliver. "I have said you shall see your daughter."

"It will not be wise to let Mr. Dagnell or my daughter know I am about to call, or that I am even in Birmingham, until I am face to face with my darling child," he added.

"I will be particularly discreet," was Mr. Oliver's reply.

" Words cannot express my—but I have said all this, and I take up your time unnecessarily," said Mr. Hilderbrandt. " Good morning, sir. I will call this evening, then, and ask for you on private business."

" Do. They'll think you have come about the robbery."

"About the what?" said Mr. Hilderbrandt. " I don't think I caught the word correctly. Did you say robbery?"

" Yes. I did say robbery, Mr. Hilderbrandt. I was robbed of several thousand pounds' worth of property last night," exclaimed Mr. Oliver. " I was burglariously broken into—I mean my house was."

" Dreadful, horrible! And do your suspicions point to anyone?"

" I can't say. I wouldn't say if I could," said Mr. Oliver, stoutly.

"This Dagnell—but there, there, I have no right to suggest that," said Mr. Hilderbrandt. " This man may be my son-in-law, secretly married to my Violet, perhaps, and I cannot cast the first stone of suspicion at him. What do the police say? Excuse me," with a low bow, "I linger—but this is strange news to me."

"Oh! the police say everything—they're very wise," Mr. Oliver answered, "they are after a boy now, who was seen on my premises last night, and I daresay they'll have him before night."

Mr. Hilderbrandt dropped his hat, picked it up, brushed it with the sleeve of his coat, and said,

"I hope they'll catch all of them. Good morning, once more, Mr. Oliver; and once more, sir, an anxious father's thanks."

He passed out of the office into the busy work-shops, from the busy workshops into the great show-room, brimming full of dish-covers and of other articles radiant with electro-silver; he bowed gracefully to one or two dapper young men on duty in the show-room; he dropped two sovereigns into a little box over which was inscribed "Workmen's Fund;" he glanced askance at a crop-haired individual, who, hat in hand, was waiting his turn for an interview with the principal, and who glanced askance at Mr. Hilderbrandt; he pushed open a pair of folding glass doors, and went down a broad flight of steps into the street, and to the carriage which was waiting for him.

There were a few loiterers about, principally children to the gutter born, and they lingered on the pavement until Mr. Hilderbandt had passed to his carriage. One boy, more officious than the rest, and bigger than the rest, ran forward and opened the door before the lacquey at the horses' heads could execute that office for himself. Mr. Hilderbrandt, smiling and courteous to inferiors, rewarded the attention with a shilling, and said,

"Thank you, my man. Critchett, Larry," he added, in a lower tone.

"I've seed him, I've been a follerin' him all the mornin'," said Larry, very quickly back again.

"You'd better cut—the slops are after you."

And, with this friendly warning, Mr. Hilderbrandt stepped into his carriage, and was whirled
away in style to his hotel.

CHAPTER XXII.

INFORMATION.

IT was the indefatigable Mr. Critchett who had been waiting in the show-room for an audience with Mr. Oliver, and it was he who was shortly ushered into the great man's presence, after Mr. Hilderbrandt's departure.

"Don't let anybody disturb us," said Mr. Oliver to the clerk, and then the doors were closed, and he gasped forth,

"Is there any news?"

"Yes, more or less, sir," was the reply; "but you've been talking about this, I'm afraid, to one of them."

"N—o, I don't think I have."

"That gentleman who has just left you now?"

"He came upon private business," said Mr.
Oliver.

"Oh! nothing to do with the robbery?"

"Nothing whatever.   Why?"

"I thought I knew him—that's all," said Mr.
Critchett, "but faces get mixed with us, at
times.   What did you say the gentleman's name
was?"

"I didn't mention his name—but it's Hilderbrandt," replied Mr. Oliver.   "Now, then, tell
me what you know, please.   You have found
out something, or you wouldn't be here."

"Yes; I've found out something."

Mr. Critchett drew his chair close to Mr.
Oliver's and began his story, which, to avoid
vain repetition in our next chapter, we will
omit from the present page.   It will suffice to
say that the revelation was a blow to the man
who listened with open mouth and widely
distended eyes, and yet a blow which he had
been preparing himself to receive all that morning.   He breathed hard, he asked many questions; he sat with his big, strong hands clutch-
ing his knees long after Mr. Critchett had concluded his narrative.

"You'll not do anything more at present—not push this, understand, until you hear from me again," Mr. Oliver said at last. "I suppose this can be done?"

"It's rather difficult, but it can be worked, I fancy."

Mr. Oliver opened his desk, and took out two ten-pound notes, which he passed to Mr. Critchett, whose willing hand slowly conveyed them to his pocket-book.

"I hate tips, but this is only paying you for your information," said Mr. Oliver, "and it's out of the common way altogether—and—and ——so on. I can always find you at the station, I suppose?"

"Yes, sir, always."

"Very good; now go away, and call to-morrow at the same time, as I may want to see you again. Good day."

"Good day, Mr. Oliver."

The officer withdrew, and Mr. Oliver sat and brooded on the information which had been imparted to him, breathing in a stertorous manner over it, and getting hotter and more

confused the more he sought to fathom its
intricacy.

"It's enough to drive one out of his senses,"
he muttered at last. "Thank God, I've got a
good strong brain of my own to bear all this."

He took the pen from behind his ear and
turned to his accounts, but the force of circumstances was too strong for him, and the hand
was soon still, and the gaze at the opposite
wall too expressive of thoughts far away from
the figures in his ledger.

"I'd rather have lost double, treble the value,
than——"

He did not finish his soliloquy, for the clerk
entered with fresh messages, to which Mr. Oliver
listened apathetically.

"What time is it?" he asked, irrelevantly.

"It's nearly one o'clock, sir."

"I shall lunch at my club, and then return
to Hagley Road. If anyone calls, say I shall
not be at business again to-day."

"Very well, sir."

The clerk was surprised. In all his experience at the factory he had not known Mr.

Oliver leave business before five o'clock, or miss a single day there. It was Mr. Oliver's pride to be always found at his post of command.

The manufacturer departed to his club, where he found his appetite fail him, and he could only look out of window into the bustling street below, instead of consuming his soup after his usual fashion. One or two friends came to him and wished to know all about the robbery, but he answered evasively, and was professedly ignorant of everything connected with it. When the questions came thick and fast, he pleaded business and hurried away, and his friends laughed behind his back at his distress.

"I should have thought the old boy would have taken the loss of a thousand or two with more composure," said one—"he's rich enough."

"It's always the way with these millionaires," said another; "touch their pockets, and their hearts bleed."

Mr. Oliver did not return home in his carriage—he had given no orders for it, and it was more easy to take a cab and be driven to Elmslie House. He stepped into the hall, hung up his hat, and walked towards the library. He asked one question of the footman who admitted him.

"Is Mr. Thomas Dagnell in the house, James?"

"He's in there, sir," was the servant's reply, pointing to the library itself.

"Oh! that's all right. I'm not at home to anybody, remember."

Then he turned the handle of the library door, and entered with a firm and heavy tread.

CHAPTER XXIII.

IN THE LIBRARY.

TOM DAGNELL was fathoms deep in the composition of a second letter to Ursula, when Mr. Oliver came into the library. He looked up and gathered his papers together as the manufacturer entered.

"You will want this desk, Mr. Oliver?" he said.

"No, keep your seat," was the reply. "I am not going to write. I," he added, after a pause, "am very glad I have found you."

"Did you want to see me in particular?" inquired Tom.

"I did."

"I am at your service, sir," said Tom, re

garding Mr. Oliver curiously now. " Is there
any fresh news of the robbery ?"

"A little.   I want to talk to you about it."

"Certainly."

Mr. Oliver drew a chair towards Tom Dagnell,
and sat down in his old attitude, only that the
hands gripped the knees hard and fast, and in
the broad face there was a sterner expression
than its wont.   Here was a duty to perform—
a more painful task than Mr. Oliver had under-
taken in all his industrious, profitable life, but he
rose to the occasion.   He had been planning
this from the time of the inspector's departure
from his office, and he thought he had sketched
out his line of action very clearly and firmly,
and was prepared for all that Tom Dagnell
might say in his defence.   He was mistaken,
however ; the young man's method of regarding matters in general, or matters in particular,
being difficult to guess at.

Mr. Oliver began well, and like a gentleman.

" Tom Dagnell," he said, in a slow, impressive
voice, " I'm not a refined or too well-educated a
man, and, if I speak too plainly for you, pray

put up with it. I will speak for your own good, body and soul, as well as I can."

Tom regarded Mr. Oliver still more curiously. He knew what was coming, but he had the strength to meet it bravely. He had never been a coward, and he knew the fallacy of the suspicions against him. He folded his letter to Ursula, and put it away in the breast pocket of his coat; he met the broad stare of his host with a pair of steady and unflinching eyes, and said calmly,

"Proceed, sir."

"It's no good brazening it out," Mr. Oliver went on; "it's no use making a worse job of what is bad enough. I don't want you to do that. I want to prove I am your father's friend and yours."

Mr. Oliver's voice broke a little, but he quickly recovered himself and continued,

"I have never had such a trouble as this in all my born days. I never thought that such a trial as this was likely to come to me. I would have given up ten thousand pounds cheerfully so that it shouldn't; because it affects more than myself—my daughter Fanny, your brother Marcus, and a heap of people I don't know."

"Well," said Tom, "what have I done?"

"You have robbed me!"

Tom Dagnell was not prepared for the occasion, after all. It came on him like a blow, despite his effort at composure, and his knowledge of the charge which would be made against him. The hasty action, the quick reply, was natural to him, yet defiant.

"It's a lie!" he answered, sharply.

"It's the truth," persisted Mr. Oliver, "and bluster won't do you any good. I had hoped you would have taken it in a different spirit—that you would have been sorry, and——"

"Stop a moment—don't run on too fast," said Tom, interrupting him. "It's no use, for it does not affect me nor apply to me. You have heard something, or been told something, that sets suspicion upon me as the robber of your forks and spoons—you have not given me credit for being above a felony. What is it warrants you in addressing me like this? Out with it, if you please."

Tom Dagnell drew his chair very close to Mr. Oliver, and looked him full in the face—there was no flinching yet.

"Ah! I'm not to be done," said Mr. Oliver, "I'm not to be put aside by bounce. I can read it all as clear as print——"

"Then, for God's sake, read out your indictment, sir, and let us get to business," cried Tom.

"I have been robbed," said Mr. Oliver, checking forth his items of accusation on his fingers, after his habit in accounts. "My house was entered by thieves, who were let in by a confederate, just as one of the gang was let into the stable yard at an earlier hour. It is more than a suspicion to connect you with the burglary—you know some of these men—you were walking about the lower part of the house at the time of the robbery, and your past character does not bear investigation."

"The result of that investigation will oblige me," said Tom.

"I haven't come from the works at this time

of day to hide anything. I'll tell you everything I heard, if not from whom I heard it," he
added, thinking suddenly of Mr. Hilderbrandt.

"We will take it that the police are your
informants—a worthy body in the aggregate,
but liable to error. Now, sir."

Mr. Oliver took a deep breath. The audacity
of the young man, his coolness, and his resist-
ance amazed him, but he was not to be deterred.
He was a brave man himself, and he thought
that very shortly the defiance would cease,
and the poor, weak fellow before him be humble
and contrite enough. He had coals of fire to
heap upon Tom's head when he knelt before
him shorn of all defence, and owned himself
to be the miserable sinner that he was.

"As for your character, you were under
suspicion from the first hour you came into the
town," continued the accuser. "For some
reason which only you can explain, you were
pursued from the railway station half round
Birmingham; you had to leave the cab you had
hired, and scale the fence of Cannon Hill Park to
elude capture; you came on here a hunted man."

"Did the police tell you this?"

"They did. They have found the cabman who drove you that night. They——"

" All this is quite true, but is irrelevant to the subject."

"It shows you are in hiding—that——"

" It proves nothing but that the cabman had a very bad horse, and I was in a hurry," answered Tom, impatiently; "all this is, at least, not your business, Mr. Oliver, and requires no explanation from me. As to my past character, now then?"

" You left home five years ago under a stigma of dishonesty. Your father charged you with robbing him, and there was a bitter quarrel, and an expulsion from the house."

"Untrue, sir," answered Tom. "I was charged, certainly, with robbing my father, but he, Heaven forgive him, has been a man of many false charges in his day. The money was not taken by me; the thief—a servant in the house—was discovered some time afterwards by my cousin Ursula. I was *not* turned away from home. I went from it of my own free will, protesting that I never would come back till I was recalled by one penitent for all the past."

"Well, well, that may be true, or may be not."

"You have only my word for it, but there is Marcus in the house."

"I wish to spare him all this—you are his brother—he is going to marry my daughter. We will not drag Marcus into this miserable discussion," said Mr. Oliver, "I will not have it."

"But I will," answered Tom, very firmly. "You have charged me with a crime—you base part of your accusation upon the vileness of my previous character. Prove that, and I will own the rest, if it's simply to oblige you," he added, mockingly.

Mr. Oliver raised and let fall his hands upon his knees; the stubbornness of human nature here was painfully apparent.

"You will deny, perhaps, you were the companion of thieves and outcasts in France?" asked Mr. Oliver.

"I was very poor," replied Tom, "I have been almost starving. Heaven knows with whom I associated in the low haunts where I was driven to exist, but I picked no pockets, broke into no man's house, coveted no man his worldly goods."

"You were in prison once."

"For a week, for shouting '*Vive la République*,' when an empire was in fashion."

"And since you have been home you have kept the company of thieves."

"You are once more mistaken," answered Tom. "I haven't a thief on the list of my visiting acquaintance."

"Ah! don't make a jest of it," said Mr. Oliver, "there's the boy you were with last night——"

"I have no proof he is a thief."

"There is the man you met on Littlehampton Sands a few days back."

"Ha!" cried Tom, "What of him?"

"You know—you know!"

"Pardon me—I do not know," answered Tom.

"You and he have planned this robbery together. Oh! it's all clear enough, and the proofs are so close at hand that your denial will avail you nothing. It's that which grieves me, Master Tom—your own hard-heartedness, your awful wickedness, your——"

"Grieve no more, Mr. Oliver," said Tom.

"What, you will own it after all? You will go away, and say how sorry you are, and I will never let a word of all this be known to anyone. I—I," he stammered forth, "have already asked the police to keep it quiet, to get on the wrong scent, to do anything rather than injure you and blast your father's good name; and if you will only say you are sorry, I don't mind my loss a ha'porth,—there! I'll lend you more money if you want it. I'll go and see your father. I'll help you to clear out of this, if you'll promise to give up your evil associates and your evil life from this day. Come, Tom, make an effort. You're a gentleman's son."

Mr. Oliver held his hands towards him, and there were tears streaming down his cheeks as he finished his appeal. In all his life he had never been thus moved—never had known such trouble for an old friend's son, for one who could have done so well for himself in the world had he wished. Tom was impressed by Mr. Oliver's earnestness, even distressed. He took the hands of the manufacturer and wrung them warmly in his own.

"I will make an effort, Mr. Oliver, but it will be to show how completely you have been mistaken in me, and in the proofs by which you have judged me. But I will not run away. I have my good name to defend, sir. You remind me that I am a gentleman's son."

He released his hold of Mr. Oliver's hands and went with quick strides from the library. He came back in an instant afterwards, and before Mr. Oliver had changed his position of amazement.

"I have brought a friend to see you, sir," he said, ushering in Violet Hilderbrandt.

CHAPTER XXIV.

CONFESSION.

WHEN Tom Dagnell had taken leave of Mr. Oliver, he had been no more prepared than that gentleman for the appearance of Violet upon the scene, and within a few seconds of the interview. As he stepped into the corridor and closed the door behind him, so there stepped from him, taken aback by his quick exit, the figure of Miss Hilderbrandt, anxious, agitated, and storm-driven.

"Miss Hilderbrandt, you here!" he cried.

"Yes, yes. I have been weak enough to listen, but it is in your cause, not my own. That is hopeless!" she exclaimed.

"But——"

"And you will forgive me for it?" she entreated. "I have been very eager to know all
that threatened you. I guessed why he had
returned when he asked for you. I saw what
was coming, and I am here to meet it."

" You must not be implicated in this."

" Pardon me, I have a story to tell. I cannot
wait for your cousin now," she said. "I have
my one friend to defend at any cost. It must
be!"

" Have you considered——"

" Everything. Take me in to see him, Tom,
for my sake, not your own."

It was the first time she had called him by
his Christian name, and he was grateful for it.
In the storm they had been drawn more closely
together.

They went in hand in hand, more like lovers
than friends; they closed the door after them,
and walked towards Mr. Oliver, who was prepared to receive them now, but wondered very
much as they approached him.

"My dear young lady," he said, very kindly,
to Violet, "I am sorry you have been dragged

into this—that he has brought you here to me."

"He has not brought me, Mr. Oliver," replied Violet, "I have brought him."

Then the three sat down and regarded each other gravely—a strange triumvirate.

"I have come to clear up a mystery to the best of my power," Violet continued, after a moment's pause. "At all events, to offer you my own solution of it."

"You may be wrong?" said Mr. Oliver.

"I think not."

"Miss Hilderbrandt, if you have no proof—"

"Let me speak of this gentleman—this one true friend," said Violet, with an imploring gesture. "I met Mr. Dagnell for the first time last March."

"For the first time?" repeated Mr. Oliver, remembering Mr. Hilderbrandt's narrative of the morning.

"I was crossing from Honfleur to England; we were passengers by the same boat. I was flying from a home where it was impossible to exist and keep honest—a bad home."

"Great Heaven!" ejaculated Mr. Oliver. "Your father——"

"Has been what the world might call a good father," said Violet. "He has given me a fair education; he has spent hundreds of pounds in developing my love and taste for music; he has surrounded me with the luxuries of life, and never given me a harsh word. He is a rich man, and has not been sparing of his wealth in my direction. I believe, even, that he has a true and fatherly affection for me."

"Then——"

"Let me finish. A few words will make it very clear to you, and free Mr. Dagnell from ungenerous suspicion," continued Violet, "and therein lies my duty, my return for his unselfish interest. I cannot consider myself when his good name is called in question. God knows, I could not be ungrateful."

"Miss Hilderbrandt," said Tom, "pray do not think of me, or add to your own embarrassments in any way. I am a strong man, you are a persecuted woman. Time will clear all things."

"The time is now," she said, almost sternly. "Mr. Oliver, my father is a receiver of stolen goods. It is his *profession*," she added, bitterly, "the one absorbing thought of his life is the study of his criminal success! He is known to the police, but has been always safe from them; he directs robberies, but takes no hand in them; they will tell you of him and his branch establishments in every city in Europe. He has made more money by his craft than you have by your honest industry."

"Dreadful! horrible!" ejaculated Mr. Oliver.

"I will not weary you with details," she continued. "It is all told in a few words. When I discovered what he was, and what an awful secret had been kept from me, when I was sure of what his life had been, and always would be, when I felt how powerless I was to save him, and that the meshes were closing slowly round myself, I ran away from home."

"I see," muttered Tom Dagnell. "It is as I thought."

"It was my mother's wish, too; and I felt

strong enough to fight my own way in the world. But I was not," she added. "My father was afraid of what I knew—of what I might betray. He thought his own child might turn informer, and drag him to prison. He set spies upon me, of which my mother warned me. He was determined to have me back, if possible. He thinks my danger is his own."

"Your danger," repeated Mr. Oliver.

"Yes. Already, by a terrible chain of fact and falsehood, I am suspected in Paris of—of diamond stealing, and there is no proof of my innocence; every proof—God help me!—of what looks like my complicity. That was my danger, Mr. Dagnell," she said, turning to Tom. "That is my danger now. I did not dream of it when I left home, and thought Heaven was helping me to go."

"It is a strange story," said Mr. Oliver.

"I would have been glad of a woman's counsel—a woman's sympathy, first of all," remarked Violet, "but the course of events has been too strong for me. You see, it has submerged him," she added, pointing to our hero.

"He came here to help me, and at my sole request. It was my father and his spies whom he wished to elude on his arrival—it was a message from my father to me that he received last night—it was in his wish to screen me that he took the part of the boy who was found upon the premises—and it was my father whom he met at Littlehampton for the first time, and who had wished to discover where I was. Ah! Mr. Dagnell, you will forgive the trouble I have brought on you, for you are generous."

"I have nothing to forgive," answered Tom. "I am only glad I understand now. I am grateful for all you have said, and at such a risk, for my sake."

"I have risked nothing."

"You have told the gentleman too much," said Tom, "and he is not too wise."

It was not meant severely—Tom had spoken half absently, and was only thinking of Violet Hilderbrandt's position, and in what way it might be affected by her revelation—but Mr. Oliver took it to himself, and answered with humility.

"No, I am not too wise," running his hands
through his scanty grey hair. "I am confused
enough. I—I don't comprehend everything,
just yet."

"Do you still think I am connected with the
robbery?" inquired our hero.

"No, I don't," he said, holding out his hand
to Tom, "and I am sorry that I ever thought
so."

Tom shook hands with Mr. Oliver again, and
thus peace, and even confidence, were re-
established between them.

"I—I don't fancy we need say anything of
this to Fanny, or Marcus, or Mrs. Oliver," remarked the manufacturer.

"No," answered Violet, "unless they——"

"Under any circumstances, Miss Hilderbrandt, we will not allude to this," said Tom,
decisively.

"A word or two more," said Violet, "and of
the robbery of last night, if you will let me
speak. The message sent me was to meet my
father's friend, whom I felt compelled to see for
a few moments—who had come to warn me of

new dangers, and how powerless they all were in any way to help me unless I returned to Paris. I do not believe my father wished to complicate matters here, or to revenge himself on those who kept me from him—by planning the robbery of this house. I think the lad who brought the message took back the news of what was in the house to his companions, and hence the burglary."

"It is a possible coincidence," said Tom.

"Only there's the picture—my Turner," said Mr. Oliver, with a groan at the reminiscence. "That wretch of a boy would have never thought of taking that. Your father, is he a judge of pictures?"

"Yes, he is," said Violet, with a shudder. "I had forgotten that."

"He is a dreadful man," said Mr. Oliver, "and he is coming here this evening."

"Here! How do you know?" exclaimed Violet.

"I promised to keep his secret—but I was deceived by him—and he did not reckon on your telling me the truth," said Mr. Oliver.

"When did you see him?" asked Violet; and thus adjured Mr. Oliver entered into a full recapitulation of the details of Mr. Hilderbrandt's visit to the factory, and of the romantic story he had invented to account for the friendship between his daughter and Tom Dagnell.

"To think of his trumping up a tale about your affection for each other—about Tom's influence over you—and you haven't seen each other half a dozen times."

. "Not half a dozen," muttered Tom, but he was scarcely certain in his mind that "numbers of times" always counted for a great deal in affairs of the heart—especially when the heart was weak, or unduly developed!

"I think we can say checkmate to Mr. Hilderbrandt now," said Tom, confidently; " his presence to-night may be of service to us."

"But he won't bring back my forks and spoons, or call with my poor Turner under his arm," murmured Mr. Oliver. " It's very natural, I suppose—but you young folk think a deuced sight more of your troubles than of mine!"

CHAPTER XXV.

WAITING.

TO a simple-minded, prosaic business-man, whose life had been that of making money by the sale of patent dish-covers, and whose chief troubles had been when rival dish-covers had risen in the market, or when the market for his own commodities had been depressed and dull, this sudden dash into the midst of love and mystery, romance and crime, was not to be desired. Beyond his little world of supply and demand, and his little hobbies of collecting china and pictures, had stretched an unknown continent of human life, of which he had known nothing, and a world beset by passions and emotions, which it would ever be beyond his powers to guage. He was satisfied with making money, and rendering home luxurious by its expenditure ; his greatest ambition was to be considered a good citizen and a man of means —he did not want anything more. Political distinction, civic distinction, a place amongst the thinkers of Birmingham—and brains work there as busily as iron wheels, and thought thrives as well as hardware—he did not desire in any way. He was not a clever man, but he had the cleverness to see that he was not clever, and to comport himself accordingly. He had known how to make a fortune out of dish-covers, and that may not be talent of the lowest order, let penniless philosophers think what they please. And, at all events, he was satisfied—that is he had been satisfied till this Tom Dagnell and this mysterious Miss Hilderbrandt had crossed the path on which he was jogging, and disturbed him, perhaps, for all time.

" I shall be precious glad when they're both out of my house," he said to himself. " To say the least, I have had a nice time of it the last two days, with one or the other of 'em." He

was still confused, it may be conjectured, by all
thåt he had heard, and seen, and suffered; he
had scarcely mastered the details, though he
had no further suspicion of Tom Dagnell, and
was sorry he had distrusted him on the evidence of an overwise policeman and a receiver
of stolen goods. Miss Hilderbrandt had been
in earnest, and had not kept the truth from him
in her anxiety to save Tom Dagnell's credit, but
the allusion to a diamond robbery was startling,
and he could see fresh complications rising very
fast about him, and himself dragged into their
midst, *nolens volens*. Then Mr. Hilderbrandt's
coming visit was disagreeable to contemplate
—the result might not be satisfactory—there
might be another scene, and he detested scenes.
Tom Dagnell might go off with a prodigious
bang again, and upset everybody's calculations.

"You purpose seeing your father," said Mr.
Oliver to Violet, at a later period, and when
an opportunity presented itself to speak to
her.

"Yes."

"And alone?'

"No," answered Violet, "not alone."

"You'll never have Mr. Dagnell with you," said Mr. Oliver; "they would come to high words, to blows—we should have a murder in the house as the next little article. We've gone in already for burglary by wholesale. All I want now is quiet, Miss Hilderbrandt—perfect quiet."

"You must come with me, Mr. Oliver," said Violet.

"God bless my soul!" he exclaimed, "and here am I trying to keep out of it all!"

"You must accompany me," she said, very firmly. "You might think presently I had not told you all the truth, and that my father was right."

"No, no, I believe you."

"You suspected Mr. Dagnell. I wonder," she added, thoughtfully, "you could have had a doubt of him!"

"Appearances were against him, Miss Hilderbrandt."

"Ay, but he is so honest and outspoken."

"Yes, he's certainly outspoken," assented Mr.

Oliver; "he said about an hour ago that I was not too wise—though, by George, it's true enough."

He broke into one of his hearty laughs at last; he was recovering by degrees. He was pleased, after all, that Miss Hilderbrandt had named him as the third party at the coming interview, though he was disposed to be nervous concerning it. It showed that she was as honest and outspoken, too, as the hero whom she defended. They were walking round the garden when this little dialogue took place, and the rest of the party were scattered.

"Well, I think I shall be a better witness than Tom Dagnell," he said, "and it will show your father there is another friend on your side."

"On my side!" she replied; "thank you for saying that. It is pleasant fo think that friends are coming round me."

"Not that I would advise you to remain here, if——"

"Yes, yes, I understand," said Violet; "I am waiting Miss Dagnell's letter to her cousin—

which may influence me more than anyone anticipates at present."

"Don't tell me anything about it," said Mr. Oliver, very quickly. "It is not my business, and—and I would rather not know anything more. You must keep these secrets and confidences for your lover, young lady; I don't want them—I doubt if I am fitly constituted to bear them."

Violet attempted a smile, but there was an expression of pain in it.

"I will not burden you with my confidence, Mr. Oliver, although I have no lover to trust," she said.

"But I presume Mr. Dagnell—though he has not seen you very often—is to a certain extent now——" and then Mr. Oliver came to full stop, feeling it was a leading question, and that the lady had changed colour, and was looking grieved and sad.

"Strange it is that everyone should think this," she said, "or dream of it. Why, sir, it would be easier to die for him than to marry him," she exclaimed, with a sudden angry impulse, which surprised her listener, and took her off her guard.

"Ah! yes, exactly—that is—shall we go back to the house now?"

"If you have nothing more to say to me," said Violet, in a different tone.

"No, nothing more at present, thank you," answered the manufacturer.

He was glad to leave Miss Hilderbrandt and escape into his library; he was more glad when it was dinner-time, and they were all facing him and looking like the quiet, every-day folk with whom he had always mixed. They discoursed upon common-place topics, and held aloof from even an allusion to the robbery, so that there should be no skeleton at the feast. In the drawing-room, after dinner, he might have thought the events of the last twenty-four hours a dream and a delusion, had it not been for the deepening lines of thought on the faces of Tom and Violet, and the signs of past depredation in the empty picture frame still hanging on his wall—a protest against felony. He was getting a little nervous himself as to the advent of Mr. Hilderbrandt; he should rejoice to see that gentleman checkmated, and all his duplicity laid bare; but he should be still happier when the interview was over, and the street-door was shut behind him who had created the mischief.

Perhaps this Hilderbrandt would not come, at the last, or suspect a trap for him, and leave the town in haste and without a word. It was close upon nine o'clock by the gilt trophy on the mantelpiece, and everybody had settled down into an after-dinner *pose*, as if nothing like romance or mystery could have existence there. Fanny Oliver and Marcus were playing chess, and there was no Slitherwick to distract the attention of either of them. Mrs. Oliver was nodding over a book; her husband had his newspaper crumpled in his lap; Tom and Violet were talking earnestly of the past or the future, and in a low tone, as befitted the gravity of a question which did not interest the others. With the old secret shivered into pieces, and at her own wish, and in his cause, there had followed a closer, sweeter confidence, just as Tom Dagnell thought there would, when faith had once been established between them. She had told him instead of Ursula, and he was glad for many reasons. She had given him time to think for her, and to plan for her.

Suddenly a knocking and ringing at the bell announced a visitor, and Violet turned pale.

"Courage," whispered Tom.

"It's Hilderbrandt," muttered Mr. Oliver.

"It's Mr. Slitherwick's knock," said Fanny, clearing off the chessmen with an impulsive elbow.

Mr. Oliver went out of the room and closed the door behind him before anyone could be announced.

"I don't like his taking the lead in this," Tom muttered to Violet; "he's a blunderer, with all his good intentions."

"We can trust him," was the answer.

"And can you trust yourself with this father?"

"Oh, yes; I am glad he has come—it is for the last time, I think."

"And you are strong, Violet? I may call

you Violet?" he said, seeing her cheek flush as
he spoke—"we are surely friends enough for
that?"

"I—I don't know."

She was looking down, and he was bending
over her, strangely fearful that he had offended
her, strangely drawn towards her by the new
ties between them, and strangely interested in
her, when the door opened, and Mr. Oliver entered with a lady.

Marcus and Tom looked up with the rest,
and exclaimed together—

"Ursula!"

CHAPTER XXVI.

THE FIRST MEETING.

IT was a mysterious coming of Ursula Dagnell, and was received in painful silence. The inmates of the drawing-room seemed taking time to understand the motive for her appearance in their midst, and guessing vaguely at it in their minds. Ursula stood there, a grave, watchful figure enough; she had stopped at sight of Tom and Violet, to whom her gaze had been at once directed, and Mr. Oliver walked on, unconscious that she was not following him.

"Polly, my dear," he said to Mrs. Oliver, "here's one you will scarcely recollect come to pay us a flying visit—here's Miss Dagnell"—

he turned and saw she had not followed him.
"Oh! *there's* Miss Dagnell, Marcus's cousin, you
know, from Broadlands."

Before the sentence had escaped him, Tom
was at Ursula's side.

"This is indeed a surprise. Is all well at
home? There is no bad news for us?" he
asked, as he shook hands with her.

"No, Tom, no bad news," replied Ursula,
"but I thought I would answer your letter for
myself, and—with myself. It was a better
plan," she added, still keeping her eyes fixed
upon Violet Hilderbrandt.

"I am very glad to see you. It was kind to
follow me like this, and will be a little change
for you; but—my father?" asked Tom.

"He wished me to start at once."

"That is strange."

"He could spare me for a few hours, he
thought," she said. "I am going back to-
morrow."

"Yes, but——"

"Presently, presently," she said, in a peevish
manner that was new to her in these new times

—"don't harass me with questions. I have to make the acquaintance of all these people, I suppose?"

"You have met them before—in the old days—with one exception."

"I do not remember them," she answered, "except this gentleman. I have seen him, I think," she added, with quiet satire.

This gentleman was Marcus, who dawdled towards her with his right hand extended.

"By gad! who would have thought of your running down to Birmingham—how are you?" inquired Marcus.

"I am very well, Marcus, thank you," she replied, shaking hands with him.

"Nothing wrong, I suppose, at home?"

"Nothing wrong," she echoed again, as she approached Mrs. Oliver, to whom she was introduced.

The introduction to Mrs. Oliver was followed by a greeting from Fanny, who was nothing if not genial.

"So glad to see you—this is an unexpected pleasure," said the manufacturer's daughter;

" we were talking of you a little while ago. I don't think I should have known you, Miss Dagnell, you have altered so much; but then, what years since I used to come to Broadlands."

" Ah ! what years ?" answered Ursula, still in the echoing mood.

Ursula turned to Violet Hilderbrandt, who had risen, and was waiting for her greeting. It was Tom who introduced them, and who watched them both with some degree of nervousness. There was much in this meeting. How would they take to each other, or understand each other from that hour?

Violet Hilderbrandt seemed waiting very anxiously, regarding the prim little figure before her very curiously, wondering even if it were possible that this was the heroine of Tom Dagnell's one romance; the woman whom he loved and was going to marry; the perfect woman in whose heart lay no selfishness, or want of charity; the woman who loved Tom Dagnell with all her heart and soul and strength, and who had waited many years for him, leaving it for time to plead in her favour

and prove the truth of her affection? So true
a woman—so old a woman!—his senior surely
by some five or six years—and this was she!

" Miss Hilderbrandt, Miss Dagnell," said Tom,
hastily, " two ladies I am very glad to see together at last."

The ladies faced each other, and the grey
eyes behind the glasses looked hard at Violet,
as though they would read her soul, if possible.

And this is Violet Hilderbrandt, thought
Ursula in her turn, the girl who had had the
power by a few words to lure Tom Dagnell
from her side and lead him into danger; who
had turned his head with the romance of her
career, and still remained a mystery to him and
the world; who was singularly graceful and
beautiful and young, with a strange pleading
face that said, " Put your faith in me," to
one who could have faith in no living woman
to whom Tom Dagnell was of interest. This
was she!

Violet Hilderbrandt stretched forth her hand
timidly, but there was no similar sign of
friendliness exhibited by Miss Dagnell, who

had been brought up in a staider, colder school. Ursula bowed in stately fashion to the younger woman, and Violet's hand fell back into the folds of her dress, and her long lashes drooped almost despairingly over the full dark eyes.

There was no word exchanged on either side, they passed from each other at once, Ursula Dagnell following the rules of ordinary courtesy, perhaps, and turning to Mrs. Oliver to address a few words to her. There was a general air of discomfort on the faces of the little community—the new-comer had not set them at their ease.

"This is your cousin," whispered Violet to Tom Dagnell, "this *is* Ursula?"

"Yes, it is Ursula," said Tom.

"I can never tell her," said Violet, very quickly.

"Miss Hilderbrandt!" exclaimed Tom.

"It seems impossible I can trust her," she continued, with a heavy sigh. "You must forgive me if I cannot."

"You will understand her presently," said Tom, "she takes a little time to understand."

"So I should think," answered Violet, doubt-fully. even mournfully, or Tom would have sus-pected satire in her answer. He was sorry the first meeting had been *apparently* a failure, for he knew well enough what a good woman Ursula Dagnell was, and how anything·out of the common way, any strange, unlooked-for trouble or affliction took her from the common way herself and made of her a heroine. She was more than generous in her estimate of human nature, and she would fold Violet Hil-derbrandt very closely to her breast when once assured of her misfortunes. It was satisfactory to think appearances *were* deceptive, and that Violet Hilderbrandt might trust Ursula Dagnell implicitly in everything. He murmured this, or something like this, to Violet in a few hasty sentences before he passed to the side of his cousin to pay her that extra degree of attention which her sudden appearance at. Elmslie House necessitated.

Mr. Oliver and Fanny were imparting to Ursula Dagnell·all the news of the robbery, Tom learned, as he approached her; they were overwhelming her with the full details of last night's catastrophe, and Ursula was listening with faint interest. So memorable an incident in a household career as a burglary, and the escape of the robbers with several thousand pounds' worth of property, did not excite the listener in the least, or arouse in her any sympathy for the misfortunes of the last four and twenty hours. She scarcely appeared to comprehend the narrative even, and although she moved her head gravely once or twice during its recital, she seemed to be far more interested in the empty picture-frame on the opposite wall.

"You are tired with your journey," said Tom to her, and this by way of a hint also to Mrs. Oliver to exhibit a little of that hospitality for which the Olivers were famous. For Miss Dagnell was still wearing her bonnet and mantle, as if prepared for a departure as unceremonious as her arrival.

"I have asked Miss Dagnell to come upstairs and take her things off," said Mrs. Oliver, as if by way of apology to our hero, "but she actually talks of going to an hotel to-night."

"As if we could allow a friend to leave us with so much room as we have to spare in the house!" cried Mr. Oliver. "No, no, Miss Dagnell, that isn't Birmingham politeness."

"Birmingham politeness hardly compels you to make room for unwelcome guests," said Ursula. "I shall be in the way here. I have no right to force myself upon you and your friends. I am one too many, I fear."

Was it fancy, or did the grey eyes flash for an instant in the direction of Violet Hilderbrandt? Pure fancy, thought Tom Dagnell, the instant afterwards.

"What nonsense!" said Tom, in a low tone, "I should not like you to go to an hotel, Ursula, and I am sure you are very welcome here."

"You are staying as a guest?" she inquired.

"Yes."

"And Miss Hilderbrandt?"

"She is a guest also."

"I think I will remain," she said, her brow contracting as she spoke, "though I did not care to be indebted to these people for any favours. I have already ordered my room at the hotel, but I—think—I will remain, Tom."

"Of course you will remain."

"If I may venture to trespass on your hospitality until the morning, then," said Ursula to Mrs. Oliver—"if I shall not be intruding too much on your kindness, I will stay?"

"That's very good of you," said Mrs. Oliver. "Fanny, you will go upstairs with Miss Dagnell."

"Oh! with pleasure."

The two ladies withdrew, and Tom sat with a somewhat thoughtful face until he found Marcus by his side.

"I say, Tom," said Marcus, "what's she come for?"

"I don't know," answered Tom—"to see for herself how we all are, I suppose."

"She has heard of Miss Hilderbrandt?"

"To be sure. What made you think she had not?" asked Tom.

"Nothing; only she looks as if she hadn't."

"Rubbish!"

"I wish she had not come," said Marcus; "I don't quite see why she has left the governor, and run down here in this deuce of a hurry. She would have been much better at home."

"It's a little change for her."

"Ye—es, exactly; but she has never cared for change, that I remember. Change," said Marcus, "does not agree with her."

"How do you know?"

"Well, of course, it's impossible to know, as she——"

He paused, and looked hard at his brother.

"Are you very glad yourself she has come?"

Tom returned his brother's fixed stare.

"I don't like surprises. I object to being taken off my guard," said Tom; "but, yes, I am glad enough to see her."

"'Pon my honour, Tom, I should not have thought it," observed Marcus, as he strolled away from his brother again. He sat down by the side of Miss Hilderbrandt, and exchanged a few words; Mr. and Mrs. Oliver remained as silent and thoughtful as Tom; presently Marcus's voice ceased also, and there was a dead silence in the room. The coming of Ursula had fallen like a blight amongst them, a few folk might have thought, judging by the external aspect of things.

"Here's another of them, Polly," Mr. Oliver muttered at last to his wife, "they're a queer lot to my thinking."

"Hush! somebody will hear you, Jonathan."

The door opened and the servant re-appeared and walked across to Mr. Oliver.

"A gentleman wishes to see you on important business, sir," he whispered in the manufacturer's ears, "the gentleman who called this morning at the works, he says."

"Show him into the library."

The servant retired, and Mr. Oliver buttoned his coat carefully, as though he were screwing up his courage with every instalment that he fastened. He walked to Violet Hilderbrandt.

"He is here. I shall be in the library. Follow me in a few minutes," he said to her, "unless you are nervous."

"Not at all," she answered, "I am quite prepared!"

CHAPTER XXVII.

VIOLET AND URSULA.

AS the door closed behind Mr. Oliver, Violet Hilderbrandt looked towards our hero, who was very quickly at her side. Marcus, full of politeness and with a due consideration for their feelings, vacated his place, and crossed to Mrs. Oliver.

"My father is here," said Violet, "and the crisis has arrived."

"I should be glad to accompany you; but you wish me not," said Tom.

"It will be as well if you take no further interest in me," she murmured.

"Why?"

"I am beginning to shadow your life, to bring

you trouble. My poor destiny, Mr. Dagnell, must lie far apart from yours, for everybody's sake," she said.

"It is too late!"

"What do you mean?" she asked.

"You saved me from a false accusation only this afternoon, and by a confession to my accuser which has wrung your heartstrings," said Tom; "do you think I have forgotten it?"

"No."

"I never shall," cried Tom; "it's just as likely that I should forget you—or anybody I respect," he added quickly, as she looked up timidly, and almost shrank away from him.

"Well, well, do not let us talk of this," said Violet; "my father is waiting for me. What if it should be my duty to give up and go back with him?"

"Oh! Miss Hilderbrandt."

"There would be the mother again," Violet murmured. "I am alone in the world here, and without a friend."

"Courage," whispered Tom; "surely there is one friend who will not fail you?"

"Yes," she answered, drawing away her hand slowly from his, which had been suddenly extended to her. "There is one, though I wish I had never sought his confidence."

"No, no! Don't say it—don't think it!"

But Violet was gone; she had passed from the room to the ordeal which was awaiting her. On her way there was Ursula Dagnell to face again; for descending the stairs together came Ursula and Fanny Oliver. Violet hesitated, stopped, and then went on again towards the former, full of a new impulse.

"Madam," she said, with tears in her dark eyes, "I am told I can trust you. You are to be my friend, he says."

"I did not come all this way to be your enemy, Miss Hilderbrandt," was the reply, but it was a marked and measured answer, and entirely free from that excitement which the younger woman was betraying. "I received your letter. I was impressed by its appeal, and I am here in response."

"And you doubt me!" cried Violet, quickly.

"I have not said so," answered Ursula. "I

have not had an opportunity to speak to you.
I am scarcely as precipitate as yourself, and do
not make friends quite so readily."

"But you are sure to like Violet," said Fanny,
" for she——"

" Miss Hilderbrandt requires no recommenda-
tion," interrupted Ursula; " if so, I have already
received one from Mr. Dagnell, who speaks in
the highest terms of her."

"And yet he knows only of my troubles—
nothing of myself," replied Violet, sadly.

" Pardon me," said Ursula, " but I thought
he did not know, and that you were waiting for
me, both of you. Unless——" she added, after
a pause, " I have entirely misunderstood the
position ? "

" Something has happened since I wrote.
It has been necessary to explain everything,"
said Violet, hurriedly.

" What has happened ?" asked Fanny. " I
haven't heard a word myself. Nobody has told
me anything."

" Patience, good friend. I have left it for
your father to relate some day. Forgive

me if I cannot tell you now," said Violet.

"I don't want to know other people's business, if other people don't care to tell me," replied Fanny, with a pout; "but if you can trust Miss Dagnell, and all at once, too, I should have thought you might have placed a little confidence in me."

"Yes, yes," said Violet, "but I am following Mr. Dagnell's advice—it is his wish that this lady should know everything."

"Oh! I didn't know Tom had wished it. Of course, what he says you will attend to," replied Fanny, almost spitefully, "but I—I don't know," —here she suddenly became hysterical—"what I have done to be distrusted by him and you like this, I—I really don't. It makes me miserable to think I—am hated like this by every— everybody!"

Fanny put her handkerchief to her eyes, and ran away down the corridor to give a little vent to her sobs before entering the drawing-room.

Ursula looked after her anxiously.

"A young woman it was certainly wise not to

confide in, Miss Hilderbrandt," said Ursula, coldly, " though why you should wish to burden anyone with troubles not of their seeking, passes my comprehension."

" I have done wrong, probably," answered Violet. " It would have been better to be silent, but I did not see all this."

" All what?" asked Ursula, as Violet spread out her hands in a strange, comprehensive fashion.

The question was asked so imperatively that Violet Hilderbrandt went back a step, as if fearful of her questioner. A minute's consideration, and then she approached Ursula more closely, and looked steadily into her face.

" *He* told me you would help me—and he has known you all his life."

" You are speaking of my cousin, I presume?" asked Ursula.

" Yes."

" And my future husband—are you aware of that?"

" Yes. He has spoken of the engagement between you."

Ursula Dagnell drew a sudden, sharp breath of relief.

"He is a man who disguises nothing," she said. "He is as quick to tell his own history as you are."

"He has been a good, kind friend to me—and I—I hope I am not ungrateful."

"Does he think you ungrateful?"

" No."

" You have rewarded his interest by perfect confidence," said Ursula, severely. " You could not keep your secret for my ears—the romance of it was for another."

" It is stern reality, not romance," exclaimed Violet, "and the shadow of it was falling upon him."

"I do not understand. Shall we——"

"You will come with me, and hear the whole truth," answered Violet, very firmly. " I read in your face that you suspect me, and I want your help, with all my heart, so much! And, yes—I *can* trust you—just as he wished I should. Come."

" As *he* wished—yes !" muttered Ursula ; but

she allowed Violet's hand to clasp her own, and
lead her towards the library, where the two men
had been waiting for some time, each wondering
what was keeping Miss Hilderbrandt away.

CHAPTER XXVIII.

FATHER AND DAUGHTER.

MR. OLIVER and his visitor were sitting a long way apart from each other; it had not been a particularly lively quarter of an hour which they had spent together in the library before the arrival of the ladies.

Mr. Hilderbrandt was a man of much forethought, and of many precautions—one who was prepared for surprises even, his path of life lying so far out of the beaten track, and skirting so closely and constantly the abyss; but for once he had been thrown out in his calculations. What was coming now he did not know himself, and was therefore unprepared for; but he was on his guard against contingencies, after Mr. Oliver's first greeting.

The man whom he had deceived so completely in the morning of that day, had received him coldly, pointed to a chair and said—

"Be seated. Your daughter will be here in a few moments. She wishes me to be a witness to the interview between you."

"But——"

Mr. Oliver checked him.

"I don't want to talk to you, myself," he said, in a louder tone, "I am quite content to be a listener. And I will not hear a word you have to say at present, knowing what you are."

"What I am! Why, that, sir," with a short, sharp laugh, "I have told you myself."

"No, sir, she has told me."

"Violet—my Violet—has told you what?"

"Everything."

Mr. Hilderbrandt looked at the stern, almost contemptuous, countenance of Mr. Oliver, and read some portion of the truth there; he was content to wait for the rest, and to consider his new position whilst he waited. He sat down, folded his arms across his narrow chest, and was completely silent until his daughter entered, and with a second witness to the interview, at whom he glanced in his old furtive way, as he rose and turned towards his child.

"Violet," he said, in a reproachful voice, "I did not expect to meet you like this. I had hoped for your old confidence in me, and you have turned against me. You—you, for whom I would have died at any time—for whom I have only lived—whom I have come to warn, to shield, and not in any way to harm, God knows. And you have told everything—you have betrayed me—you have trapped me into this!"

The man's voice trembled as he spoke, and there was no histrionic passion in his outburst, only the true exhibition, for once, of the feelings which were in him. It was easy to believe that this pariah loved his daughter, and was stung deeply by the fact that she had told the secret of his life to those who would betray him to the French galleys, or the English prisons,

were it in their power. It was incomprehensi-
ble to him—he thought he had known his daughter better.

He dropped into the chair from which he had
risen, and clasped his hands together.

"Why did you do it? You cannot bear me
any malice. I have been so proud of you,
Violet," he continued, "I have tried so hard to
make your life happy and keep the troubles
from you. Why have you told these people
about me?"

It was his one reproach. He could not
understand a motive for his daughter's action.
He had come full of deceit himself, and with
many lies on his lips, but it was for her sake,
not his own. He cast away now all semblance
of the character which he had intended to
assume—Violet Hilderbrandt was before him,
and she had betrayed him. From his own point
of view, it was a base ingratitude; he could
scarcely realize it even now.

"I have defended myself. I have defended a
friend against unjust suspicions," answered
Violet, "and the innocent had no right to suffer

for the guilty. But I have not betrayed you, father; neither this gentleman nor lady will repeat a word I have said."

Mr. Hilderbrandt's black eyes wandered from the gentleman to the lady alluded to, then he muttered—

"What *have* you said? Let me know the worst. I do not suppose I shall attempt to contradict you. What does it matter"—here the black eyes blazed forth with a new fire— " what becomes of me ?"

" I have told everything for the sake of the one friend I have in this world——"

" Who is that ?" asked her father, interrupting her.

" Mr. Dagnell."

" Ah ! yes, always this Mr. Dagnell," said Hilderbrandt, savagely, " go on."

" They would have accused him of being in the robbery that occurred last night," Violet continued ; " many things had happened to cast suspicion upon him, and I could only explain them by a confession of the truth."

" What do you call the truth ?" said Mr.

Hilderbrandt, "out with it, girl—I am not ashamed of it myself."

"I have told the whole story," said Violet, firmly, "how I left home as soon as the awful fact struck me that you were not honest— that you were dragging me down with you, and making me—against your will, perhaps— your accomplice. But still your accomplice— your own daughter !"

Mr. Hilderbrandt took a little time to consider the position again. His appeal had failed to stir his daughter's heart; his reproach had not disarmed her; the evidence of his affection had not made her swerve from the resolution which she had formed. The game was up; the trouble was over; the daughter was for ever lost to him; he must think of himself and his own safety after this.

"I will own that suspicions have been against me," he said, "but there are no proofs, and I could have explained a great deal if you had listened, and not run away from Honfleur with your lover."

Ursula Dagnell winced.

"If you think Mr. Dagnell is my lover, it is one more mistake," Violet replied. "I saw him for the first time in my life on the night I ran away from home."

"It may be true though appearances are against you, but I will believe it if you say so," remarked Mr. Hilderbrandt.

"I have already said so," was the calm reply.

"Very well, I am satisfied," Mr. Hilderbrandt continued. "You have been always truthful, quick to judge, awfully quick to condemn, but I have never known you tell a falsehood. I accept your explanation, Violet. I have not another word to say."

Mr. Hilderbrandt had ingeniously shifted his ground—he had become almost the party wronged ; but his listeners were on their guard, and not impressed by him. He was aware of this, and he turned from his daughter to Mr. Oliver.

"Mr. Oliver," he said, "it is my proud satisfaction that I have not in any way sought to deceive you."

"That's a good one, that is," replied Mr. Oliver.

"I may have deceived myself, for it was natural to imagine my daughter had eloped with Mr. Dagnell, when the first news I received from a servant of mine, who was one of the crew on that occasion, was of her crossing with this Mr. Dagnell from Honfleur to Littlehampton," said Mr. Hilderbrandt, "when I trace her to Birmingham and find Dagnell with her here, in your house, when now at least he is everything to her, and I am nothing! It is all a folly most unworthy of her—it is a madness which puts faith in him, and turns away from me. I said so at your office, sir—I repeat it in your home."

"Look here," said Mr. Oliver, bluntly, "I am not to be done twice, old fool as you may think me. Are you a receiver of stolen goods or not? Have the police been watching you for years?"

"God forbid!" said Mr. Hilderbrandt, very piously and heartily.

"Your daughter has, to your knowledge, never told a falsehood," said Ursula Dagnell, at this juncture.

Mr. Hilderbrandt started at the clear, cold, cutting tone of voice which now addressed him.

"I do not know this lady," he muttered; "I have not the honour."

"I am Mr. Dagnell's cousin," answered Ursula for herself.

"I was not prepared for you—I was promised a private interview with my daughter, but Mr. Oliver has broken faith with me. There is," he added, with a sigh, "no trusting human nature."

"I thought you a man of honour when—no, dashed if I'll make any excuses!" exclaimed Mr. Oliver, "and you may think yourself lucky—I say lucky—that, out of respect to your daughter, I don't hand you over to the police."

"Sir, you have no power—there is no charge against me," said Mr. Hilderbrandt, rising and drawing himself up, very straight and rigid; "I defy you and your police altogether. Were there not ladies present, I would say—damn your police!"

"You had a hand in last night's burglary—you know you had."

" I know nothing of it."

" You'll make a fine thing out of the plate, but what the devil are you going to do with the Turner?"

" I don't comprehend what you mean," said Mr. Hilderbrandt, and if his bewildered look were assumed, it was exceedingly well done. "I don't know any turner. I am completely in the dark; but before I go, I will mention one thing."

" Well, sir, well," said Mr. Oliver, " look sharp, I have lost all patience with you."

"I stated this morning that myself and my partner were general merchants. We sell and buy with half the world. We are no hole-and-corner firm, sir; and jealous folk—Heaven forgive them all!—have spread reports to our prejudice, and, as you see, have even turned my daughter against me. What she believed, I cannot ask you to discredit," he said. " I will go away under this painful stigma, and will pray for your enlightenment some day."

He walked towards the door, paused, shuffled with his feet, looked round with very restless eyes, and then, putting his hat on his head, went slowly back to his daughter's side.

"Good-bye, Violet," he said, in a more natural tone. "You will say good-bye to me?"

"Yes; good-bye."

She put her hands in his, and he held them very close and firm.

"My mother—is she well?" asked Violet, in a low voice.

"No, far from well."

"If—if she could come to me! Oh, if you could part with *her!*" said Violet.

"Impossible," said Mr. Hilderbrandt. "She is a true woman, and will not desert me."

"Poor mother!" whispered Violet.

Mr. Hilderbrandt stooped, paused, and kissed his daughter, who did not shrink away from him.

"Good-bye, once more," he said. "If you had stopped with us, all would have been well. For what will happen now blame yourself, *not* me. I came from France to save you. - So help my God, for nothing else!"

"I will try to save myself," murmured Violet.

"I came to warn you," he whispered, "to

hide you from them all. There is a warrant out for your arrest, as I feared there would be. It was signed this afternoon, in London. Get away from here."

" Is this true?" asked Violet.

" As the Gospel," answered her father; " you must disappear, or be brought on to Paris. Here is money—a roll of notes—take it."

" No, no, I will not touch your money!" cried Violet, shrinking from him, and speaking in a louder voice. " I will not have it—I have said so."

" Well, well, Heaven help you, if the father must not!"

Thus this strange father and daughter parted, and Mr. Hilderbrandt went from Elmslie House without another word. There was no effort made to stay him; conscious of his own safety, he marched away with chest square and head erect, whilst watchful eyes were on him, but in the darkness of the Hagley Road the head drooped slowly, the chest contracted, and the shoulders were raised almost to the ears, as he skulked on his desolate way.

Presently a man stole from the opposite side of the road towards him.

"Hilderbrandt!" said he, hastily.

"Ah! Jardine," was the reply, "is that you?"

"Won't she come back?" was the eager question. "Has she given us up?"

"Yes, the lot of us," was the answer, "and I don't care how it ends now."

"What folly!"

"By all that's holy, I don't!" cried Hilderbrandt. "Poor Violet, poor girl, if I could only have got her out of the way!"

"We must get out of the way ourselves, and pretty soon too," said the other.

Meanwhile, Violet had sunk into a chair, and sat like one struck into stone. Her father had gone, the storm was coming on, and she was helpless. The world was very black and dim; she did not know where she was—there were thunderous noises, as of the sea, in her ears and at her brain—and she floated away into a dim, vague world, where nothing seemed to live. She had fainted again, as on the night of the

ball.   When she came to, it was Ursula Dagnell who was at her side—the shimmer of the
light upon her glasses was the first fact of which
she was conscious.

"Courage," said Ursula in her ear, "you are
with friends."

"Do you believe in me, then?" she asked,
faintly, yet anxiously.

"Yes," answered Ursula.

CHAPTER XXIX.

THE NEW FRIEND.

VIOLET HILDERBRANDT'S strength did not return that evening; even the assurance of Miss Dagnell's new faith had no power to bring the colour to her cheeks. The crisis had come, the worst was known; the whole truth seemed to have given her new friends and brought her peace of mind, but she remained very weak and ill. If the ship had reached the harbour, the storm had shattered it sadly. What of the oncoming storm which it must sail out to meet again? And what of the preparations to meet it?

" You are far from strong yet," said Ursula to her, half an hour after Mr. Hilderbrandt's departure. "Will you not go to your room?"

"If you will come—if you will sit with me for a little while," replied Violet, almost imploringly.

"Would you not prefer the company of Miss Oliver?" asked Ursula.

"No. I have much to explain to you now," replied Violet.

"Yes—now!" answered Ursula. "But why not leave this till the morning? I can guess what has occurred. I have heard all."

"Ah! but I want you to understand me as well as my history," said Violet, earnestly; "and, pardon me, Miss Dagnell, but I wish to know more of you, and your goodness."

"Have they told you how very good I am?" asked Ursula, sadly, and yet with a ring of satire in her sadness.

"He has."

"My cousin Tom, you mean?" inquired Ursula.

"Yes."

"It is kind of him to sing my praises. I

cannot do it for myself," said she, and a heavy sigh escaped her, which was not to be repressed.

They were sitting in the library still, and Violet's hand was resting on Ursula's, which it had sought the instant after the recovery from her swoon. Mr. Oliver had crept away on tiptoe and left the ladies to themselves; he was glad to get from them before anything fresh should arise to implicate him in the matter. He was disturbed by Miss Dagnell's sudden appearance, and, in his nervous condition, already scented danger from afar. Let him keep well out of it this time, and get these combustible atoms out of his house, too, as speedily as possible.

"They who are the best and kindest, are always ready to protest against any goodness in themselves," said Violet, thoughtfully. "Even in my little experience of life, I have learned that one fact thoroughly."

"You must not attempt to flatter me," replied Ursula, coldly, " for what you find in me may disappoint you very much. I am not a perfect woman—I have many enemies, and only one friend."

" And that one is——"

"The gentleman to whom I am engaged, and who told you of his own free will of our engagement. I think you said so, Miss Hilderbrandt?"

Ursula spoke like a woman still in doubt as to the truth, and still perplexed by it.

" Yes," answered Violet, " he told me of his engagement."

" We will go together to your room, if you wish," said Ursula. " We shall be quiet there, and I shall have time to think what is best for you—and for all of us," she added, after a moment's further consideration, as though the position needed it.

Confidence being thus established between them, it seemed to Violet Hilderbrandt that the clouds were lifting, and that presently, with Heaven's help, there might be light upon the path she was pursuing. The sense of the dangers of which her father had warned her receded into the background, now that she was

not utterly alone. There were strong, brave
friends at last to re-assure her, to fight her
battles, and teach others to believe in her as
they had done themselves. Ah! strange cir-
cumstance of life, let her say fate, even!—that
lucky journey across sea in the wild March
morning, when she ran away from home, and
met Mr. Dagnell on board the Littlehampton
steamer.

In the seclusion of her own room, she spoke
a great deal of this Mr. Dagnell, and with that
warmth of gratitude for the service he had
rendered her, which he would never allow her
to express in his presence. She could speak of
him now, she thought, to one who understood
him so well, and loved him so truly, as the pale-
faced little lady there; Ursula Dagnell would
be glad to listen to his praises from her lips,
for she knew what an honest, earnest man he
was.

Ursula listened very attentively, but the face
was set and grave, as though there were more
pain than pleasure in remaining silent. She
did not discourage the recital; on the contrary,

when the conversation seemed to flag a little, a leading question or two escaped the thin, closed lips. Violet forgot her weakness, and Ursula Dagnell did not remind her of it again. The younger woman was under analysis—under the microscope—and the elder was in search of truth, or of a flaw in the character of her to whose rescue she had been summoned. Weak or strong, in sickness or in health, it was necessary to understand Violet Hilderbrandt for good and all—even for evil and all—if this were a plot to lead him she loved into temptation. There might be Tom Dagnell's battle to fight as well as her own, for what she knew to the contrary. She had left Broadlands that morning resolving to see and act for herself, and meet this mystery full front.

It was not readily that the set expression of Ursula Dagnell's countenance gave way, but there came a change to it after a while, and the grey eyes showed more womanly sympathy and interest.

"May I ask how old you are?" Ursula said, suddenly.

"I am eighteen years of age."

"So young!" murmured Ursula. "So very young to face the world."

"I am looking much older now. I have had so much to think about, to plan, to fight against, that I often fancy I am turning grey. Don't you think I look more than eighteen?" she asked.

"I thought you might be twenty possibly, but then I have not seen you at your best," replied Ursula. "You have been troubled; this day has been a trial to you."

"I am not sorry it has come; I am glad it has passed, if it leave you a friend of mine?" said Violet, timidly.

"I am a poor hand at making friends, as I have told you," replied Ursula, less warmly. "I take no more quickly to strangers than strangers take to me."

"That is because there is not time, perhaps, but I seem to know you now so thoroughly and well."

Ursula shivered a little as though she were cold, and it was a very forced smile with which she answered her.

"Mr. Dagnell has given me too good a character," she said, "as he was in duty bound to do, but still the picture is flattering and the colours are not my own with which he has painted me. God knows that!" she added, with a sudden warmth and earnestness that was particularly striking after her previous coldness of demeanour. Violet leaned forward in her chair and looked closely into the faded face of the elder woman. She was amazed, but she hardly knew in what way to reply. Still she hazarded an answer, and it had been better unsaid, despite the flattery it unintentionally conveyed.

"He is not likely to have been deceived in you," said Violet.

"Why not?" was the quick rejoinder; "men and women deceive each other very often—of their own free wills or against their natural convictions—deceit is more common than uprightness. Surely you have found it so, Miss Hilderbrandt?"

"Ah! but my life has been wild and unreal," was the sad answer.

" So has mine," was the sharp, short comment
here.

" Miss Daguell, you——"

" I think so," said Ursula, interrupting her,
" for I have met with many surprises in my life.
Even my engagement to my cousin is as wild
and unreal as anything that could have happened to me. We seem hardly a match, I daresay ?"

" I can guess why he loves you, " replied
Violet.

" I am older than he by some three years. I
am a plain woman—we have quarrelled half our
lives away," said Ursula, with her hands clasped
tightly together, and with her gaze fixed
steadily on Violet.

" Still he loves you—what does it matter ?"

" You understand this, you say ?" inquired
Ursula. " It seems natural to you ?"

" Yes—very natural."

" Do you understand, too, why I love *him* ? "
was the next inquiry.

" Oh ! yes," cried Violet, more readily, and the
colour deepened unconsciously in her face, and

the light glowed in her dark eyes, as she replied.

"People have talked against him very much," Ursula continued. "He is always hasty, and not always just. He is brusque, unpolished, and at times uncharitable; he says bitter things without much regard for others' feelings, and he makes enemies quickly. His own father and mother cannot be said to care for him, and would not shed a single tear if he were dead to-morrow."

"But they are very hard and eccentric, I have heard."

"So is he."

"I have not noticed it," said Violet; "he has been always considerate and open-hearted. Surely one more unselfish does not exist—a better or more honest gentleman seems impossible to me. But you know all this so well, for you love him. You see behind the little mannerisms of his character how true a heart he has."

"I am the only one who has seen it—save yourself," said Ursula.

"How strange!"

"Yes, very strange, or very natural, I don't know which," replied Ursula, speaking rapidly now; "but I understand him, and I am as proud of my love for him as of his love for me. I could die for him very willingly, just as the women do upon the stage, and just as stagily, and I could strike down anyone who tried to take his love away from me, as surely as any tragedy queen who ever mouthed before the footlights."

"Who would be cruel enough to attempt it?"

"There is nothing crueler than a woman, the satirist says," Ursula remarked; "and I am inclined to believe him very often."

"That is a creed I will not follow you in, Miss Dagnell."

"I will not ask you, at your age," said Ursula, in reply; "but we Dagnells are a strange race, and not a little revengeful. Tom is revengeful at times."

"Impossible!"

"I thought he was as revengeful and unforgiving as the rest of us, but I was deceived," said Ursula, " for he came back with no malice in his heart against us. And, perhaps, in his place, I should have kept away for ever."

" He was in the right, then ?"

" He was treated infamously by all of us."

"Tell me the whole story, please," said Violet, eagerly.

"Not now. It is late," replied Ursula, " and we have been together too long."

" Ah ! yes," said Violet, with a sigh, "I am keeping you away from him."

" Have *you* no lover ?" Ursula inquired ; " it is a plain question on a short acquaintance; but I will ask it, if you will allow me."

" Neither lover nor true friend until I came to England."

" And then ?"

" And then I found true friends."

" And no lover ?"

" And no lover," replied Violet. " What could I do with him ? How could he marry one whose life has been submerged as mine has," she cried, " and who, at any moment, may pass into the shadow again ? Oh, Miss Dagnell, I want peace, not romance."

" We will try to secure it for you."

" Heaven bless you for that assurance," said Violet, "I am very glad you are my friend."

" You doubted me at first ?"

" N—no," replied Violet, hesitatingly, " at first I thought—that——"

It was difficult to explain, and Violet came to a full stop.

" People always dislike me," said Ursula, very calmly. " I am not surprised at your first impression of me, Miss Hilderbrandt. And I came here full of doubts of you, and showed them quickly."

" They are dispelled now ?" asked Violet.

" They are all gone, I think—I know," said Ursula, and then with a sudden impulse, she stooped forwards, kissed her, bade her good night, and left the room.

When Ursula was seated in the drawing-room by the side of Tom Dagnell, she said to him—

" I have seen your heroine."

Tom did not reply. He waited anxiously for his cousin's verdict.

" And like her," she added.

" I am glad of that—I knew you would," cried Tom, enthusiastically.

" And will believe in her," continued Ursula, " so long as she is fair with me."

" Do you doubt——"

" She is very young, she is more of a child than a woman. I do not comprehend how one brought up as she has been can be so artless and unaffected. And," added Ursula, " her virtues are not assumed, that I can see."

" I'll swear they are not," cried Tom.

" And you are a judge of all that is excellent in woman," said Ursula, in so strange a tone that Tom took time to reflect upon his answer. His own reply was apt enough and complimentary at last, but it had lagged on its way a little.

" Or I should not have been so fortunate in my choice of a future helpmate," he said, gallantly.

The face softened at the compliment, and

there were strange and sudden tears behind the crystal.

"God bless you, Tom," she murmured. "We will take care of this child, for a time. I have been afraid of her—of your—of your coming down here at all. But my heart has grown stronger lately—much stronger!"

Thus Ursula Dagnell's mission had been a complete success, and thus the drop scene falls on pleasant groupings and perfect confidence all round, as in the last act of the play when the audience is shuffling to the portals and the green curtain is going down for good.

But this is only the end of an act, and of more acting than these "principal characters" were aware at the time.

BOOK III.

MISERERE.

CHAPTER I.

THE NEW HOME.

IT was fair summer weather at Broadlands when the cousins brought home Violet Hilderbrandt. It was a strange time for visitors, but this was a strange visitor to match, and one who was to give nobody trouble. Tom and his cousin left Elmslie House the next morning, with Mr. Hilderbrandt's daughter in charge. It seemed a wise and politic measure to get away from Birmingham, and Mr. Oliver entirely agreed with them, and was only too ready to place his carriage at their disposal for immediate conveyance to the station.

Fanny Oliver shed many tears at Violet's departure, begged she would write to her, and promised to write herself—" Oh ! almost every day !"—and Marcus shook hands fishily all round, and sent his respectful compliments to his parents, and an intimation, to all whom it might concern, that he should be back on the tenth of June next, and please see that his room was ready and his bed carefully aired.

The journey from Birmingham to Little-hampton was accomplished without any incident by the way, and it was in the misty even-time that the three travellers were driven along the broad carriage-drive to the entrance doors of Sir John Dagnell's mansion.

"This is your home," said Violet, "you should be happy here, you two."

" We have found happiness of late days," was Ursula's answer, " or a something like it," she added, with a reserve.

Tom did not respond. His mind was busy with other thoughts; he had gone away in haste, and left a father sick unto death, and he would not have been surprised now to find the blinds down before every window of the great house. Only a few days ago since he had departed, and yet what a new lifetime it had been, and how full of changes and surprises! He did not know how many; he had not the courage to dwell upon one great change, one cruel surprise, of which the proof might rise some day against him like a ghost out of its deep grave. He was sad and thoughtful, as he looked towards home, and Ursula, quick to observe, said,

"What are you thinking of, Tom?"

"Of a hundred things," was his evasive answer; "all of which are too mixed up for explanation at present. This is the home from which I ran away," he said, turning to Violet; "I always feel the shadow of it resting like a weight on me when I approach the place."

"I was not aware you disliked Broadlands in itself," said Ursula.

"I shall not be sorry to get clear of it," Tom replied. "The house will fall to Marcus's share, not to mine, I suppose, and I rejoice at it. But, by Jove! here I am thinking of the poor old governor's possessions, after all my protests!"

The welcome to Broadlands was not wholly unfriendly, although partaking of a mixed character, at which Violet Hilderbrandt might have wondered in her heart. The servants came into the hall to do them reverence, with old Robin Fisher at their head; and the grave, set visages which accompanied their bows to Miss Dagnell were the more marked by contrast with the beaming smiles bestowed in the direction of the young master. Cabbage, who formed one of the arrival party, slouched into the hall with his tongue out, as though conscious of some burlesque in the welcome home, and stretched himself full length upon the hall mat, immediately the door was closed, as if glad to get back and be once more at his ease.

"How is my father, Robin?" were Tom's first words.

"A leetle fretful—not getting on quite so well with her ladyship as with Miss Dagnell, perhaps, Master Tom, but tolerably well, considerin'," said the butler, after a moment's grave reflection on the subject; "he's pretty much as you left him, take him in the lump."

"Well, that is good news," said Tom. "I will go up and see him."

"I will join you in a few minutes—when I have shown Miss Hilderbrandt her room," said Ursula. "Tell Sir John I will not be long."

"My mother——"

"Lady Dagnell has gone to Arundel for a drive," explained Mr. Fisher.

"She is well, of course?" asked Tom.

"Her ladyship is very well," replied Robin. "I think I heard her say she would be glad when Miss Dagnell returned to help her nurse Sir John, as he was uncommon trying; but still her ladyship is very well."

"Has she been much in attendance upon him?" asked Ursula, with sudden interest.

"She was with him quite five minutes yesterday," said Robin, dryly, as he moved slowly away with his hands crossed behind his back. He did not withdraw wholly from the hall, however, for, as Ursula and Violet went up the broad stairs, he stepped forward again and touched our hero on the arm.

"May I take the liberty of asking who that

is now?" he said, in a husky whisper, "it's a strange face, Master Tom."

"And has no right to be here without your permission—eh?" said Tom, laughingly.

"I don't mind that," was the reply. "You needn't be hard on me. I'm glad to see it for that matter," said the butler.

"Why?"

"It's a nice face," said Fisher—"it's a bright, wholesome sort of good looks that will light the place up. Who is the lady?"

"Miss Hilderbrandt; a friend of Miss Dagnell's," answered Tom.

"Miss Hil—and Miss Ursula's friend too. Did you say Hilderbrandt?" asked the old man, as if in doubt still.

"Yes, I said Hilderbrandt," replied Tom. "You told me once the name was familiar to you."

"And I told you why. Does Sir John expect the lady?"

"I am going to inform him she is here," and Tom went up the stairs to communicate the tidings to his father. He was not quite satisfied with Mr. Fisher's manner, but the old butler was garrulous, and Tom thought he would not tell him that this was the daughter of the Paul Hilderbrandt of whom he had once spoken.

Tom knocked lightly for admittance at the door of his father's room, and Mrs. Coombes was quick to respond.

"We heard the wheels, sir," said she, with a little bob of her portly person at the sight of our hero; "and Sir John thought it must be you and Miss Dagnell back again."

"He is about the same, I hear?"

"He is dreadful fidgety this morning," said the nurse, in a low tone—"restless and peevish —awful! But," in a louder key, and evidently for the edification of the patient within the apartment, "this way, Mr. Dagnell; you will find Sir John looking quite well and strong again."

"That's no reason you should bawl like that," piped the querulous voice behind the screen. "Come in and say what you have to say—don't make that noise outside."

Tom entered at this crude request, shook

hands with his father, who sat crouched in his chair before the fire, despite the summer that was upon them now, in the same attitude as he had left him a few days ago. It was as if he had sat there all the time waiting for his son's return.

"Ah! you have thought fit to come home again?" said Sir John, bitterly. "It did not seem quite seemly for the father to die alone, like a rat in a hole."

"I am sorry if my absence has disturbed you in any way, father," replied Tom. "I understood you did not object to my departure."

"You did not say what you were going off in such a hurry for," grumbled Sir John; "you pretended it was to see Marcus."

"You know, then?"

"As much as Ursula thought it worth her while to tell me," said Sir John—"that there was a woman in the way, and she was not going to stand that sort of thing. What the devil have you been up to, Tom? Can't you open your mouth, now you are back? What woman is it?"

Tom was considerably astonished, but he said, calmly,

"A friend of mine—a friend of Ursula's."

"Ursula never had a friend—don't tell me that," was the quick reply.

"A friend of Ursula's," repeated his son, "whom she has brought back to spend a few days with her."

"Ursula has brought back *that* woman ?"

"That *lady* is with her now," said Tom, with emphasis. "We thought the change would do her good, as she has been far from well, and not free from trouble. I will tell you the whole story, if you wish."

"I don't want to hear anything about it," Sir John answered. "I don't care for a parcel of strange people in the house, but, if you keep her out of my way, I shall have nothing to say until I get downstairs again. Ursula will look sharp enough after her for all of us, I'll wager —though what she has dragged her here for, the Lord only knows. What does your mother say to the arrangement?"

"My mother is not at home."

"Ah! it's no matter what she says," he remarked, "she's never twice alike with her tempers. She has led me a fine life since you and Ursula sneaked off, coming in here with her complaints, as if I had not enough of my own to irritate me. Is Marcus back?" inquired Sir John.

"He will extend his stay another week."

"I don't want him—he was never like a son to me," muttered Sir John; "if I had my way, I'd cut him clean out of my will to-night. Is old Oliver well?"

"Very well."

"I'm sorry for that," observed the sick man —"a little of my affliction would do him a deal of good. It would take some of his abominable pride down. I hate people who flaunt their riches in your face. Where is Ursula?" he asked, suddenly.

"She will be here in a few minutes."

"I never said she wouldn't," replied Sir John; "I asked you where she was."

"She is with Miss Hilderbrandt."

Sir John Dagnell's lower jaw dropped, and

he remained open-mouthed for a while, with his eyes glaring at his son.

"Miss Hilderbrandt," he said at last—"that is—the name of the young woman—who has been brought into my house?" There was a difficulty in getting his words out, and his breath had become very short and quick. Tom Dagnell did not fail to notice the change in his parent at the mention of Violet's name, although he refrained from any comment. He said simply,

"Yes, that is the name."

"Is she a foreigner?" asked Sir John, "for I hate foreigners."

"Her father is a German, her mother an Englishwoman."

"Where does she come from?"

"Paris."

"Ursula did not tell me her name was Hilderbrandt," muttered Sir John; "not that it matters to me what her name is, but still one does not care to be kept in the dark as to all that is going on in his own family. Perhaps she did not know?"

He waited for an answer to this question from his son, and Tom, remembering the telegram which had summoned him to Birmingham, said,

"Yes, Ursula knew the lady's name."

"Before she left Broadlands to join you?" said Sir John, still singularly persistent on the point.

"Yes—before."

Sir John twisted his fingers together and cracked every joint unpleasantly, but he did not answer for awhile. When he spoke at last, the same topic was evidently troubling him.

"Ursula was in too great a passion, I suppose, to remember anything save that you were love-making on the sly," said Sir John; "that's like her—when she once fires up, there's no doing anything with her."

"Was she very much excited at my letter?" inquired Tom.

"She would not stop in the place another minute, she said; she walked up and down, up and down this room and the corridor, and went on like a mad woman," was the father's answer, " anyone would have thought she had escaped from an asylum, or that you were something awfully scarce and precious. And to go on like that, and excite me in my weak state. That was a kind and charitable proceeding, wasn't it ?"

" Probably you said something to irritate her, sir ?" suggested Tom, whose heart had grown heavy during the last few moments. " Ursula does not readily lose her self-command."

" I remember saying something about you— I don't know what it was now, but it was said in my usual calm, good-tempered sort of man- ner—and she raged like a tigress, and said she would go to Birmingham at once, and I might die, and be damned, for what she cared. No, I think *I* made that last remark, when she began to aggravate me."

" I did not know there had been any differ- ence between you. Surely it was unnecessary," said Tom.

" Yes, Tom, it was quite unnecessary !" said Ursula's voice, so close behind them that both father and son started. "I am still more sorry that Sir John should have mentioned it."

"It does not matter," Tom answered. "'All's well that ends well.'"

"He told me he would not speak of it, but"—with a severe glance in the direction of the invalid—"it is only one more breach of faith between us."

Sir John Dagnell winced as though she had lashed at him with a whip. He was completely cowed and submissive; he had not one word to urge in his defence.

"I had forgotten, Ursula," he whimpered. "I am extremely sorry, but Tom began his infernal questioning, and wormed the whole truth out of me. I am too credulous and simple for this world, and it is that which makes me fear sometimes I shan't get over my attack."

"I daresay I was excited at leaving Broadlands in hot haste," said Ursula, thoughtfully. "I scarcely remember. I was very anxious to get away, and it is possible I was jealous,

Tom, of your interest in anyone whom I did not know, and whom I had never seen. You are not angry with me? I *was* very, very unhappy."

"Angry, Ursula—no. But I hardly understand——"

"Don't try. All is past, and this is the beginning of the new life," she said, earnestly. "I see it shining on us."

"'Tis a fair prospect in the light," Tom answered, as he rested his hand upon her shoulder, "and we will not trouble ourselves with the bygones!"·

He went out of the room, and left uncle and niece together. Ursula sat down in the chair which he had vacated, crossed her hands in her lap, and looked at the sick man almost wearily.

"Well," she said, "have you anything to ask me?"

"You did not tell me her name was Hilderbrandt," he said.

"It was as well not."

"Surely not *his* daughter in this house?" he asked, eagerly.

"Yes, his daughter."

"Paul Hilderbrandt's?"

"Paul Hilderbrandt's!" she echoed.

"Why have you brought her here?" was his next inquiry. "Tell me that."

CHAPTER II.

SIR JOHN IS NERVOUS.

THE old City knight and his niece dropped their voices to a whisper, as though listeners might be lurking in the background, and matter of grave moment to themselves were to be discussed. There was no one near. Tom had gone downstairs, and Mrs. Coombes had been sent out of the room by Ursula a few minutes since.

Still these two were careful folk, or the low tone which Sir John had assumed had been followed, as if in unison, by Ursula.

" Why have I brought Violet Hilderbrandt to Broadlands ?" said the niece. " Is that a reason so difficult to guess ?"

"It is to me," replied Sir John. "What is the use of it?"

"Have I not always been eager to know the best, or worst?" she said. "Have I been afraid of the truth?"

"I cannot say you have."

"It is better to know the worst and get it over," muttered Ursula. "You," she added, contemptuously, "have been always fearful of the truth, and see what it has ended in!"

"We have not got to the end. You were very hard upon me," he complained.

"On the contrary, I was very merciful."

"Well, well," said the old man, restlessly, "don't let us go over that matter again. As Tom says, 'Bygones are bygones,' and you bear me no ill-will now the bargain between us is concluded."

"I bear you no ill-will," she repeated, slowly.

"You have been very kind to me, I will say that," he added; "almost a real daughter, and that is why I am anxious about you."

"Go on."

"And that is why I ask for what reason you

bring this girl here?" he said. "Would it not have been better to keep her away, if Tom has fallen in love with her?"

Ursula's hands were clenched, as she replied,

"I have no evidence he is in love with her— she tells me she is not in love with him. I want to have faith in the honour of them both. I want," she added, more warmly, "to live down the meanness, the jealousy, and the terrible distrust which have blighted my whole life."

"In your place I would have kept her away."

"I should be glad of some woman to love," said Ursula, thoughtfully. "I should be happier with one woman's true affection for me, and I am weak enough to think that I may be able to secure it."

"Why?"

"Tom has spoken well of me," was the reply. "She trusts me."

"Tom does not know your true character," said Sir John, thoughtfully. "If he only knew you——"

Ursula's quick hand fell upon the wrist of her

uncle, and gripped it so hard and fast that he cried out with sudden pain.

"Think of that again—hint it by a single word—and what is your life worth to me, do you think?" she hissed in his ears.

"Good God! you would not kill me," exclaimed her uncle.

"If I thought you would break your promise, and turn Tom against me,—if I could dream of so much treachery, you would be found lying dead in your bed before the morning," said Ursula, calmly.

"I don't think of betraying you, of course not," replied her uncle. "Heaven forbid, but I am very weak. Why do you upset me like this?"

"It is your own fault. We were speaking of Hilderbrandt's daughter, not of Tom," said Ursula.

"Ah, yes; Hilderbrandt's daughter. What a coincidence, or what a plot against us! It is just because she is Hilderbrandt's daughter that I am afraid of her."

"Afraid !"

"Some of her father's cunning has surely fallen to her share," replied Sir John.

"I do not believe it."

"You want to believe the best of everybody now," said Sir John, sarcastically. "That is your new creed."

"I will try, at any rate."

"You will be on your guard, though?" he asked.

"I am never off it," was the answer.

"Very good," said Sir John, with a croaking little laugh; "we can trust you not to walk about with your eyes shut—short-sighted as you are."

"Tom wishes me to be Violet Hilderbrandt's friend," said Ursula. "It is my duty, my pleasure, to study every wish of his, and at any sacrifice."

"And supposing—mind you, I only say supposing—Tom falls in love with this girl?" asked Sir John, "are you prepared to sacrifice yourself for her happiness?"

"No."

"For Tom's happiness?" was his next inquiry.

"It is too late."

"How is that?"

"When he went away I offered him his liberty, and he would not take it. I would have borne all misery then; I was prepared for it. He assured me of his love—he tells me still of his affection—I believe in him! But——"

"But?" repeated Sir John.

"If he has deceived me, he must bear with the result," Ursula concluded, moodily. "There will be no mercy."

"No, you are not particularly merciful," said Sir John, with a steady stare at the red coals; "and it will serve him right, whatever happens, after all that he has promised. I shan't care; he has never been a good son to me; I never liked him. If it hadn't been for you, he would have been starving now in France—he——"

"We know all that," said Ursula, interrupting him, "and how you do not deserve to have a son grow up to love and honour you, or to forgive you, as he has done, for all your gross injustice, and the sins of your mis-spent, awful life. Don't say a word against him," she cried, in a higher key, " or I shall strike you, helpless as you are."

"I will not say another word," remarked Sir John; "I want to be the best of friends with you—with all of you. We have forgiven everything; we're quite a happy family now !"

" I love your son, and never again will I hear you speak against him."

" He's a tolerably amiable fellow, now and then," said Sir John; "and I have only wished to intimate that he may want looking after, with a pretty woman, in whom he is interested, in the house. That's all. I know I should, at any rate."

" You !" said Ursula, contemptuously.

" I don't mean now, but when I was a good-looking fellow," said Sir John; "and I only fancy that it was not wise to bring the girl here."

" It was Tom's wish," she said again.

" Yes—but Tom may suffer for it presently—

and a nice disturbance there will be if——"

Again she interrupted him.

"Tom may not suffer—it will be the other one !"

"Eh—what other one ? You mean——"

Ursula rose.

"I have no more to say," she remarked. "Tom and I call this the beginning of the new life—with the light upon it, and the clouds in the background for ever. I try to see that also. I want to have faith in humanity, in human motives, in myself again ! Don't crush me utterly with doubts. I am trying to be good. I am praying to be worthy of your son—do you see ?—do you hear ?"

"Yes, yes—exactly. Good morning. You had better take a walk in the grounds now, or Tom will wonder at your excitement. I don't want another scene—I am weak, remember."

"I will send Mrs. Coombes to you."

"You are very kind to me, Ursula. Pray send her—I don't care to be left quite alone. Send some one ; anyone will do—but *you !*" he added to himself, as Ursula passed out of the room, and he lay back cowering in his chair, as if new fears had come to him with his niece's revelation of that morning.

CHAPTER III.

THE RUNAWAYS.

THE late May glided into the warm days of
June, and it was bright summer weather
at Broadlands.

Peace and rest seemed to have settled on a
home where peace and rest had never been till
that time; and halcyon days had surely come
at last, despite, or possibly on account of, the
long illness of Tom's father.

Those who saw Sir John every day did not
note much change in him; he was "no better
and no worse," it was affirmed by Mrs. Coombes,
by Ursula, and even by the doctors. It was Sir
John's own opinion also that he was stronger,
and should be down with them all again soon, the

blessing that he thought he was to home. But there were one or two wise folk in Sussex who saw more clearly to the end, and prophesied concerning it.

Old Robin Fisher, a bird of evil omen, croaked his doleful notes below stairs, and Lady Dagnell was already resigned to her future widowhood, and talked of it as very close at hand.

"The old master gets more like a shadow every day, but they don't see it, or they won't," Mr. Fisher opined. "He wastes fast, just like his father did—just like I shall, one of these fine days."

"Will Mr. Marcus make a better master?" asked one of the footmen.

"He can't make us a worse," remarked another.

"He's dying like a heathen, too," said the cook, who was of a pious turn, and went regularly to the Roman Catholic Church, at Littlehampton. "Nobody to confess him, priest or Protestant—it's awful."

"It's the only 'sistent thing he's done," Robin

Fisher remarked; "for he has lived like a heathen all his life."

"Ah! you know more about him than you care to tell us, Mr. Fisher," said another servant.

"It's uncommon likely that I do."

"And what keeps you about so late at nights, Mr. Fisher, creeping up and down the stairs, and outside his room especially? Do you mind telling us what that's for?" asked a saucy page, who had no respect for grey hairs, and was intensely curious.

"Who says I do?" asked Mr. Fisher, taken aback at this charge.

"I've seen you—so has Tilda."

"If you and Tilda can't keep your tongues between your teeth, you're not long for Broadlands service," said Mr. Fisher, very much aggrieved, "and what you and Tilda want together in the passages after—but there, I'm not going to lose my temper."

The page laughed, and the servants laughed in chorus with him. Mr. Fisher was not held in any esteem by his subordinates, and service was not hard to resign at a moment's notice, or without a moment's notice, in this establishment.

"I'll tell you what I'm about,—I've nothing to conceal," said Mr. Fisher, when the merriment had subsided, "I'm waiting, patient and quiet, for the worst. I should not like to be out of the way when Sir John goes off for good. I'm always round the corner—ready."

"Don't you go to bed at all?" asked footman No. 1.

"P'raps I do, p'raps I don't," was the enigmatic answer, "I only say I'm ready and waiting."

"Well, I wish you had not told me," said the cook, "I've had the creeps enough since I've been here without your adding to them. If I'd come sudden-like upon you in the upstairs passages, you'd given me a fit."

"Your place is in your room," said Mr. Fisher, loftily. "No one will ask for you, or think of you, when Sir John goes off."

"Nor you either," was the ready retort.

"I'm not quite sure of it," replied Mr. Fisher,

"and, at all events, I'm ready for the asking."

This talk of the servants' hall occurred some three weeks after the return of Tom Dagnell to his father's home. Violet Hilderbrandt was still a guest there, and Marcus had been back two weeks from Birmingham. Life went on in much the same way as usual, although Violet had made a difference in the house, and was a different being in herself. She had confessed in Birmingham to an ignorance of home and of home comforts, of happy faces, or honest lives about her, and dull as Broadlands might be it was a new sphere of existence for her—a haven, as we have already intimated, where, at least, she might rest and gather strength.

They were all friends about her—even Lady Dagnell had learned to like her, as she had never liked anyone till that time, and would have had her for a constant attendant on her whims and caprices, had not Tom put a veto on his mother's selfishness. There was Ursula to confide in also—a new Ursula, as frank and friendly as she had imagined her to be before they had met at Elmslie House, a warm-hearted

being, prone to sudden fits of reverie which
were difficult to dispel, but who had faith in her
now and would not hear of her leaving Broadlands yet awhile, until she—a clear-headed
woman—had sketched forth the future life.
There was Marcus, also, full of a grave courtesy
towards her, though saying little and wondering more at her friendship with his cousin
Ursula; and there was Tom Dagnell, always
bright, and strong, and self-reliant, like some
dear brother whom she had found late in life,
and whom she could hold very high in her
esteem without a thought of danger. Sir John
Dagnell she had never seen, or been allowed to
see. It was a strange thought that, of the
absent host cowering in his room away from
her.

"He is too ill," said Ursula, " what is the use
of knowing him ?"

"I can hardly explain," said Violet, " but I
should like to see Tom's father."

"He does not resemble Tom, in any way,"
was the reply.

Violet did not admire the tone of the answer

she received, but Ursula was kind the rest of
the day, and in the evening they walked together along the sands, with Tom as attendant
cavalier, and Cabbage in the background. That
was a memorable evening—it marked an epoch
in their lives—it began their lives anew from
that night.

They had walked towards Littlehampton.
The tide was going down, and a long stretch of
sand lay before them. The sun was setting
gloriously, as it ever seems to set on this part
of the Sussex coast, and the sky was aflame
with such golds and crimsons as no painter had
put to canvas yet. They were as happy as
such folk could be; they had turned their backs
on Broadlands, and their thoughts away from
it, and Tom was at his best and in his highest
spirits—spirits that were strangely high, even
for one who had always looked at life with a
laughing face, and been defiant of its tragic
aspect. They were close on Littlehampton
when a lady and gentleman from the opposite
direction advanced towards them, too much
absorbed in each other's conversation to take

heed of their approach till they were close upon them. It was Cabbage, eternally observant and with a memory for faces that would have made the fortnne of a detective policeman, who was the first to recognise them, and who, with a grateful remembrance of a friendly pat or two from the gentleman, and a handsome contribution of party fragments in a Dresden china plate from the lady, suddenly barked forth his welcome and plunged towards them with all the force at his command.

The gentleman jumped and the lady scream-ed in the first instance; then they stooped and caressed Cab's big brown head, and finally, after some whispered words together, as of mutual self-assurance, they turned towards Tom and the ladies.

"Miss Oliver—Mr. Slitherwick!" exclaimed our hero.

The astonishment depicted on the countenance of Tom Dagnell added to the embarrassment of the lady and gentleman, after greetings had been exchanged between them.

"Haven't you received my letter?" asked

Fanny. "Oh! dear—has not Marcus got it yet?"

"If Marcus has received a letter, he has said nothing about it," answered Tom.

"This is very dreadful—I was sure he—Oh, dear, dear, what shall I do, Edwin?" she exclaimed, turning to Mr. Slitherwick and clasping both hands upon his arm. "Advise me what to do? I have only you to trust in now!"

Fanny began to whimper, and Mr. Slitherwick patted her hands gently with his own.

"Courage, my precious darling, courage," he said. "It is easily explained—we have come to Littlehampton to explain, you know. Don't grieve—some of these good friends will sympathize with you, I am sure."

"I—I—did not expect to meet them," sobbed Fanny; "I didn't wish to see them like this— all of a row! Oh! to what bitter suffering I am justly exposed. Yes, Mr. Tom—Violet— Miss Ursula, I say justly! Poor Marcus, too, who I hoped would come to me to-morrow, all forgiveness. Oh! dear."

"This gentleman is your husband?" asked Tom, very sternly.

"Yes—yes—yes—that's it," said Fanny, "we have been married the last three days, by spe—spe—special licence. Edwin, tell them everything, I cannot bear this ordeal. Look at his accusing face! Ask him to spare me."

"I have no accusation to make—I have nothing to say," said Tom, "only this. Is Marcus to meet you?"

"To-morrow morning, on the esplanade—half-past nine," murmured Fanny.

"You had better reserve all communications till then," said Ursula, very frigidly, "and allow me to wish you a good evening."

"Violet, you will stay with me—*you* will bear with me—you will not judge too hastily?" exclaimed Fanny, as Ursula Dagnell turned to retrace her steps towards Broadlands. "I loved you—I have not treated you badly— I have written to you this afternoon such a long letter! You haven't got that, I suppose yet?"

"No," said Violet, bewildered by Fanny's

excitement, and by the news which she had heard. "I am very sorry—that is, I am very much surprised. I cannot leave Miss Dagnell to go back alone." .

"If Mr. Dagnell would allow me to explain," said Mr. Slitherwick, "in a few words, too, I should take it as a favour."

"Perhaps it is as well. I shall see Marcus when I return," answered Tom, thoughtfully. "Violet, will you join my cousin ?"

"Yes, pray join her," said Fanny, "and let us hear from you soon. We shall be at the Grand Hotel, Paris, next Saturday. Good-bye, dear. Heaven bless you !"

Violet went away with Fanny's blessing on her head, and Cabbage, after looking from her to Tom, and being uncertain what to do on his own account under this divided sense of duty, sat down on the wet sand and whined softly to himself.

"Shall we walk on ?" suggested Mr. Slitherwick. "The sand is damp, and——"

"I would prefer to remain where we are,"

said Tom, moodily, "your explanation will not take very long?"

" Not very, but——"

" Give me the plain facts, which I can offer to my brother, and spare me your comments, please," said Tom.

"All I can spare you I will," replied Mr. Slitherwick, "and I hope you will see with me and my dear Fanny that what has happened is for the best."

" I think that already."

" Oh! that is generous of you, Tom. It is like you," exclaimed Fanny, looking out of the white handkerchief in which she had buried her countenance.

"It is very much for the best that my brother has not married you. He will think so too," continued Tom, "unless he is weaker than I fancy."

" You see, Mr. Dagnell," said Mr. Slitherwick, " my Fanny never loved your brother. She tried all she could after her rash engagement, but your brother was cold, unsympathetic, un-

congenial. She had offered to release him—
she has asked almost to be released herself—it
has ended in one false reconciliation after another, and this is the result."

"So I perceive."

"Mr. Oliver—Mrs. Oliver would not interfere
—they were all against her, and we loved each
other passionately," Mr. Slitherwick continued.
"Matters were approaching a climax, and I
could not see this dear girl sacrificed, and all
her happiness scattered to the winds of heaven.
The affection of the heart over-ruled the cold
contract of society—we fled! We were married at Brighton a few days back. We may
have acted rashly, Mr. Dagnell, but we cannot
say we repent the step which we have taken.
That would be a treachery to ourselves."

"Is this the speech with which my brother is
to be favoured to-morrow?" asked Tom, quietly.

"No, sir," said Mr. Slitherwick, more loftily.
"Fanny will see him, tell him everything, and
ask his forgiveness."

"What do Mr. and Mrs. Oliver think of this
proceeding?"

"They have bowed to the inevitable."

"And the inevitable is very much obliged to them," said Tom, "and so ends the story. Well, Fanny," he added, turning to the young bride, "you might have treated poor old Marcus better, and told him you loved this gentleman, and not his dreamy self. It would have been less romantic, but more straightforward."

"I—I didn't know what to do, Tom ; I didn't indeed," sobbed Fanny, "and I was very miserable. Don't reproach me. I had hoped for your sympathy. I—I thought *you* might pity one who was tied down to an old promise before she knew her own mind."

Tom felt that a dagger had struck him at these words, whether intended to wound him or not, but he did not betray any discomposure.

"I don't judge you," he answered, "I only blame you for the silly way you have gone to work."

"What would you have done in my place?"

"I would have told Marcus the whole truth— he would have readily cancelled the agreement."

"The whole truth is not so easy, Tom," she answered. "You will find that out some day for yourself."

Yes, she had meant the stab for him, she had judged him as one in the toils, and, though his colour changed this time, he did not waver from the position he had assumed.

"At all events, when the day comes I will face the worst, not run away from it," he answered, gravely.

"I have seized the first opportunity to meet Marcus," said Fanny ; "and to ask his pardon. I shall be always unhappy without it. Mr. Slitherwick and I will stay at Littlehampton till he comes to me with his forgiveness, if we stay for ever!"

"You will find it a dull place for a long stay, I am afraid," was Tom's reply; then he raised his hat to man and wife and strode from them at a quick pace, anxious to overtake his cousin and Violet Hilderbrandt. But they were a long way ahead of him, mere specks along the distant sands, and it struck him at last that it was difficult to reach them before they turned towards Broadlands, and that his anxiety to come up with them was growing less with every step he took in their direction. Presently he had slackened his pace, and was proceeding with his head bent down, and the thoughts within him deep, and strong, and bitter. He did not care for company now; he should be glad if those ahead of him reached Broadlands first, and gave him time to think it out.

Poor Marcus, so badly treated and so lightly set aside! And poor Fanny, so frivolous, and hasty and romantic! It was as well it all ended thus, perhaps, but they might have wound up their story with a shade more grace, and a little more consideration for one left out in the cold. It was quickly over, certainly. There was some rough philosophy in ending this burlesque of love by a *coup de main;* it saved the feelings in the long run, but for all that it was a terribly unceremonious, heartless, cruel truth. Still it was the whole truth, and the woman he had left on the sands with her husband had told him that the whole truth was not easy to face, and that there would come a day when he would find it out for himself! Had he found it out already, on that very day when the young wife's words had stung him in his apathy, and roused him into active thought and fear? The crimson and gold glories of the day had vanished now; the sky was of a dull dead slate colour, and there was a moaning out at sea as of some one lost and despairing;—it sounded like a woman's voice to him as he plodded on across the sands in the deepening twilight, and thought of the story which had been told him there. He could only mutter to himself, "Poor Marcus!" but there were heart echoes in that hour that gave back ominous answers to him.

CHAPTER IV.

A LITTLE STRANGE.

WHEN Tom Dagnell reached Broadlands he found Ursula waiting under the portico of the house. The door was open, and Violet Hilderbrandt had passed in and disappeared. It was the woman to whom he was engaged to be married who was lingering there for him.

"It has been a long story, Tom," Ursula said, as he approached; "shall you repeat it to Marcus to-night?"

"I think so," said Tom. "Is there any reason for delay?"

"Such a pitiable tale will keep," she replied; "and your brother might be spared till the morning."

"Do you think it will affect him in any great degree?"

"Yes."

"We have never given Marcus credit for much feeling," said Tom, "and I do not care to hide this from him. I would rather tell him in my own way than leave it to that foolish girl's letter to explain."

"I have no great faith in Marcus's feelings, as you know," she replied, "but I would spare him till the last. It is so sudden and mysterious, and if he ever loved anybody but himself, it was that pink-faced fool we met to-night," she cried, indignantly.

"I am glad you feel for Marcus, Ursula; he has not had many troubles in his life, but this is one, I think."

"I feel for anyone pushed aside out of a fair pathway into the thorns and brambles. Tell him to thank God, Tom, he is a man!"

She laid her hand upon his arm in her excitement.

"Men may suffer as well as women, Ursula," said Tom.

"Ay, but they are strong, and shake off trouble quickly. I don't think," she added, "any care sinks into men's hearts—men's souls, as into weak women's. Do you?"

"Yes, I do," answered Tom. "Not that Marcus is going to fret his life away."

"As a woman might. You own that?"

"As a weak woman might; but not a brave one with pride in herself."

"She might collapse too," murmured Ursula.

"Her strong common sense would tell her it was for the best. Just as this is for the best that Marcus should not have married a woman who cared nothing about him," said Tom.

"What have you on your mind to-night?" asked Ursula.

"Nothing," answered Tom, quickly. "We are only arguing as to the relative mental strength of the sexes."

"And, like most debaters, we are of the same opinion still," said Ursula, lightly. "Come, let us console Marcus together, if you are determined to tell him to-night."

"But you——"

"I am curious to see how he will take it; I am anxious," she added, "to contribute my little amount of consolation, if it's necessary."

Tom did not admire the suggestion; he could not see that Marcus would care for the consolation of one who had never offered consolation to him in her life—who had satirised and almost despised him, in the old crabbed days of her discontent, not so very long ago. He had faith in Ursula, but he could not see any good to follow her introduction upon the scene, and he felt that, with her as a witness, he should not be at his best, or Marcus either. It was strange how deeply he felt for his brother at this crisis, and how closely he seemed drawn towards him.

"You must let me see Marcus alone, Ursula," he said, when they were in the hall, and Tom had learned from the footman that his brother was upstairs in his room.

"As you please," replied Ursula, stopping suddenly.

"I don't fancy you could do any good, or

that any woman's sympathy would do him good just now," said Tom, in explanation.

"And that I may do more harm than good, you mean?"

"It is not impossible. Marcus is an odd fellow, and takes things oddly."

"Like his brother," was the ready answer; "and, after all, I was perhaps more curious to see you than console him?"

"Why?"

"I don't know. I can't tell you," she replied, evasively; "go to Marcus, and I will find Miss Hilderbrandt. Ah, how strange!"

"What is strange?" asked Tom, pausing with one foot upon the stairs.

"All *is* for the best perhaps. Marcus is free," she said, very quickly, "and this Violet Hilderbrandt will make him a good wife, Tom, if you and I are match-makers enough to bring it about. It would not be a grand match for Marcus. Sir John would consider it a *mésalliance*, but she is a simple gentlewoman, and would suit him very well. Why, she may even already love him! '*Les femmes sont si étranges,*' the Frenchman has said.

"Violet and Marcus!" said Tom, with a loud laugh. "Oh! that is too ridiculous—it is impossible!"

"You don't know—how can you tell?"

"You have taken this matter deeply to heart, Ursula," he said. "Your cheeks are flushed, and your breath is short."

"It is the cold wind from the sea," she replied, shuddering.

"The whole affair has distressed and excited you."

"Perhaps it has," she answered. "I am going to Violet now. She is sorry for Marcus, and thinks he has been treated very cavalierly. Pity *is* akin to love, Tom!"

Tom shook his head almost angrily.

"I am tired of this foolish theory. We are not quite off with Marcus's old love yet," he added. "I have to announce its dissolution first."

"Yes," was the reply, "and I would rather be this brute, Tom," pointing to the large dog which had stretched himself at full length, in his favourite attitude, on the hall mat, "than Marcus Dagnell to-night."

"Marcus will bear his trouble bravely, like a Dagnell," replied Tom, as he walked upstairs, leaving Ursula in the hall with her hands clasped, and her gaze directed towards him, as though the sight of him were hard to part with, or there was a spell upon her—upon them both —in that hour.

As he turned the bend of the stairs, his backward glance assured him she was looking at him still; he smiled and waved his hand towards her, but she did not respond to his signal, or smile back in return. He had been a little hard, perhaps, and she was offended with him ;—he did not know what he had said, he was uncertain what she had said to him, or what had been implied. There was a vague fear in his mind even that Violet and Ursula's return to Broadlands had not been without some grave discussion of Marcus's case, and that something had been said not wholly tending to perfect harmony. Why did Ursula look after him in that strange way—almost as if she had learned to doubt him with the rest of human kind about her? Why had she wished to accompany him in search of Marcus, too, and hear his explanation of the case?

He was revolving this, and more than this, in his mind, when he knocked at the door of his brother's room, and Marcus from within called to him to enter.

END OF THE SECOND VOLUME.

LONDON: PRINTED BY DUNCAN MACDONALD, BLENHEIM HOUSE.